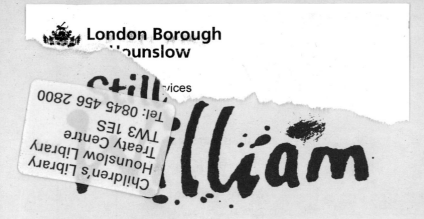

stilliam

Richmal Crompton was born in Lancashire in 1890. The first story about William Brown appeared in *Home* magazine in 1919, and the first collection of William stories was published in book form three years later. In all, thirty-eight William books were published, the last one in 1970, after Richmal Crompton's death.

'Probably the funniest, toughest children's books ever written'
Sunday Times on the Just William series

'Richmal Crompton's creation [has] been famed for his cavalier attitude to life and those who would seek to circumscribe his enjoyment of it ever since he first appeared'
Guardian

Still William

RICHMAL CROMPTON

Foreword by Sir Tony Robinson

Illustrated by Thomas Henry

MACMILLAN CHILDREN'S BOOKS

First published 1925
This selection first published 1984 by Macmillan Children's Books

This edition published 2016 by Macmillan Children's Books
an imprint of Pan Macmillan
20 New Wharf Road, London N1 9RR
Associated companies throughout the world
www.panmacmillan.com

ISBN 978-1-4472-8557-1

1 3 5 7 9 8 6 4 2

A CIP catalogue record for this book is available from the British Library.

Typeset by Nigel Hazle
Printed and bound by CPI Group (UK) Ltd, Croydon CR0 4YY

To Colonel R. D. Crompton, C. B., R. E.

CONTENTS

FOREWORD

FIVE BRILLIANT THINGS ABOUT WILLIAM

1. He Has a Field at the Bottom of His Garden

When I was a boy, my cousin Colin lived in a small country town, and there was a field at the bottom of his garden. It was enormous and overgrown, with a rusty car in one corner that you could sit in and pretend to drive, and a very grumpy goat tethered to a post, which would butt you if you got too close. There were two other children, a boy and a girl, who lived three doors down, and sometimes they were in our gang, and sometimes they were the enemy. I've always wanted a field like that.

2. He Is Very Good at Climbing Trees

In the small back garden of our house in London there was an apple tree. I used to climb up to the very top and squidge the long lines of ants that busied themselves in the branches. I thought I was really brave, like an explorer planting his Union Jack on top of Mount Everest.

I went back to visit that house recently, and the apple tree is still there. It's not really very tall at all, in fact it's not much bigger than a large bush. William is much braver than I ever was. In the chapter called 'A Bit of Blackmail' he seems to climb really high – but maybe he's just fooling himself.

3. He Is Kind to Most Animals

There are two types of people – those who like animals and those who don't even seem to notice them. William is the first sort of person, and he especially likes his dog, but isn't very keen on his cat or some insects. In fact he can be pretty mean to them. But who am I to judge: I used to squidge ants.

4. He Acts Out Brilliant Stories

When I was a boy, I thought I was a rebel leader. Every time I flushed the toilet I'd get shot in the back by a government sniper. I'd stagger out of the loo and into the bathroom, barely managing to wash my hands as the life ebbed from me. I'd stagger across the landing, teeter at the top of the stairs, then roll, slide and tumble down them groaning in agony, until I finally came to rest by the front doormat, where I lay dead, a tragic waste of a young life. Then my mum would shout, 'Breakfast, Tony!' and I'd get up and go into the kitchen for a fried egg or beans on toast. William does that sort of thing, only a million times better.

5. He Is Very Serious

Let's face it, most adults are pretty idiotic – at least, William thinks so. They dress weirdly, behave weirdly, tell people off for no good reason, and even when there is a good reason they tend to tell off the wrong person. When they talk to each other they laugh a lot – that high-pitched, nervous laughter that doesn't really mean anything. But William isn't a laugher. He knows what's important – his gang, playing at pirates, getting muddy, capturing insects – and he takes these things very seriously. What has he got to laugh about? When he's playing he's got a serious responsibility as leader of the gang, and when he's at home someone or other is always having a go at him. And anyway when he does laugh he sounds like a braying donkey.

The first William book was written nearly a hundred years ago. The word 'cool' hadn't yet been invented. Well, it had, but only in the sense that your hot chocolate's cool if you forget to drink it for half an hour. But the writer Richmal Crompton knew William was cool, and tens of thousands of readers down the decades have known the same thing. All boys want to be like William, and not just boys – grown-ups do too. I certainly do. Why do you think I agreed to write this intro-duck-shun? (That's how William would spell 'introduction'.)

Sir Tony Robinson

CHAPTER I

THE BISHOP'S HANDKERCHIEF

Until now William had taken no interest in his handkerchiefs as toilet accessories. They were greyish (once white) squares useful for blotting ink or carrying frogs or making lifelike rats to divert the long hours of afternoon school, but otherwise he had had no pride or interest in them.

But last week, Ginger (a member of the circle known to themselves as the Outlaws of which William was the leader) had received a handkerchief as a birthday present from an aunt in London. William, on hearing the news, had jeered, but the sight of the handkerchief had silenced him.

It was a large handkerchief, larger than William had conceived it possible for handkerchiefs to be. It was made of silk, and contained all the colours of the rainbow. Round the edge green dragons sported upon a red ground. Ginger displayed it at first deprecatingly, fully prepared for scorn and merriment, and for some moments, the fate of the handkerchief hung in the balance. But there

1

was something about the handkerchief that impressed them.

'Kinder – funny,' said Henry critically.

'Jolly big, isn't it?' said Douglas uncertainly.

''S more like a *sheet*,' said William, wavering between scorn and admiration.

Ginger was relieved. At any rate they had taken it seriously. They had not wept tears of mirth over it. That afternoon he drew it out of his pocket with a flourish and airily wiped his nose with it. The next morning Henry appeared with a handkerchief almost exactly like it, and the day after that Douglas had one. William felt his prestige lowered. He – the born leader – was the only one of the select circle who did not possess a coloured silk handkerchief.

That evening he approached his mother.

'I don't think white ones is much use,' he said.

'Don't scrape your feet on the carpet, William,' said his mother placidly. 'I thought white ones were the only tame kind – not that I think your father will let you have any more. You know what he said when they got all over the floor and bit his finger.'

'I'm not talkin' about *rats*,' said William. 'I'm talkin' about handkerchiefs.'

'Oh – handkerchiefs! White ones are far the best. They

launder properly. They come out a good colour – at least yours don't, but that's because you get them so black – but there's nothing better than white linen.'

'Pers'nally,' said William with a judicial air, 'I think silk's better than linen an' white's so tirin' to look at. I think a kind of colour's better for your eyes. My eyes do ache a bit sometimes. I think it's prob'ly with keep lookin' at white handkerchiefs.'

'Don't be silly, William. I'm not going to buy you silk handkerchiefs to get covered with mud and ink and coal as yours do.'

Mrs Brown calmly cut off her darning wool as she spoke, and took another sock from the pile by her chair. William sighed.

'Oh, I wouldn't do those things with a *silk* one,' he said earnestly. 'It's only because they're *cotton* ones I do those things.'

'Linen,' corrected Mrs Brown.

'Linen an' cotton's the same,' said William, 'it's not *silk*. I jus' want a *silk* one with colours an' so on, that's all. That's all I want. It's not much. Just a *silk* handkerchief with colours. Surely—'

'I'm *not* going to buy you another *thing*, William,' said Mrs Brown firmly. 'I had to get you a new suit and new collars only last month, and your overcoat's dreadful, because you *will* crawl through the ditch in it—'

William resented this cowardly change of attack.

'I'm not talkin' about suits an' collars an' overcoats an' so on,' he said; 'I'm talkin' about *handkerchiefs*. I simply ask you if—'

'If you want a silk handkerchief, William,' said Mrs Brown decisively, 'you'll have to buy one.'

'Well!' said William, aghast at the unfairness of the remark, 'Well, jus' fancy you sayin' that to me when you know I've not got any money, when you *know* I'm not even *going* to have any money for years an' years an' years.'

'You shouldn't have broken the landing window,' said Mrs Brown.

William was pained and disappointed. He had no illusions about his father and elder brother, but he had expected more feeling and sympathy from his mother.

Determinedly, but not very hopefully, he went to his father, who was reading a newspaper in the library.

'You know, Father,' said William confidingly, taking his seat upon the newspaper rack. 'I think white ones is all right for children – and so on. Wot I mean to say is that when you get older coloured ones is better.'

'Really?' said his father politely.

4

'Yes,' said William, encouraged. 'They wouldn't show dirt so, either – not like white ones do. An' they're bigger, too. They'd be cheaper in the end. They wouldn't cost so much for laundry – and so on.'

'Exactly,' murmured his father, turning over to the next page.

'Well,' said William boldly, 'if you'd very kin'ly buy me some, or one would do, or I could buy them, or if you'd jus' give me—'

'As I haven't the remotest idea what you're talking about,' said his father, 'I don't see how I can. Would you be so very kind as to remove yourself from the newspaper rack for a minute and let me get the evening paper? I'm so sorry to trouble you. Thank you so much.'

'Handkerchiefs!' said William impatiently. 'I keep telling you. It's *handkerchiefs*. I jus' want a nice silk coloured one, 'cause I think it would last longer and be cheaper in the wash. That's all. I think the ones I have makes such a lot of trouble for the laundry. I jus'—'

'Though deeply moved by your consideration for other people,' said Mr Brown, as he ran his eye down the financial column, 'I may as well save you any further waste of your valuable time and eloquence by informing you at once that you won't get a halfpenny out of me if you talk till midnight.'

William went with silent disgust and slow dignity from the room.

Next he investigated Robert's bedroom. He opened Robert's dressing-table drawer and turned over handkerchiefs. He caught his breath with surprise and pleasure. There it was beneath all Robert's other handkerchiefs – larger, silkier, more multicoloured than Ginger's or Douglas's or Henry's. He gazed at it in ecstatic joy. He slipped it into his pocket and, standing before the looking-glass, took it out with a flourish, shaking its lustrous folds. He was absorbed in this occupation when Robert entered. Robert looked at him with elder-brother disapproval.

'I told you that if I caught you playing monkey tricks in my room again—' he began threateningly, glancing suspiciously at the bed, in the 'apple pie' arrangements of which William was an expert.

'I'm not, Robert,' said William with disarming innocence. 'Honest I'm not. I jus' wanted to borrow a handkerchief. I thought you wun't mind lendin' me a handkerchief.'

'Well, I would,' said Robert shortly, 'so you can jolly well clear out.'

'It was this one I thought you wun't mind lendin' me,' said William. 'I wun't take one of your nice white ones, but I thought you wun't mind me having this ole coloured dirty-looking one.'

'Did you? Well, give it back to me.'

Reluctantly William handed it back to Robert.

'How much'll you give it me for?' he said shortly.

'Well, how much have you?' said Robert ruthlessly.

'Nothin' – not jus' at present,' admitted William. 'But I'd *do* something for you for it. I'd do anythin' you want done for it. You just tell me what to do for it, an' I'll *do* it.'

'Well, you can – you can get the Bishop's handkerchief for me, and then I'll give mine to you.'

The trouble with Robert was that he imagined himself a wit.

The trouble with William was that he took things literally.

The Bishop was expected in the village the next day. It was the great event of the summer. He was a distant relation of the Vicar's. He was to open the Sale of Work, address a large meeting on Temperance, spend the night at the Vicarage, and depart the next morning.

The Bishop was a fatherly, simple-minded old man of seventy. He enjoyed the Sale of Work except for one thing. Wherever he looked he met the gaze of a freckled untidy frowning small boy. He could not understand it. The boy seemed to be everywhere. The boy seemed to follow him about. He came to the conclusion that it must be his imagination, but it made him feel vaguely uneasy.

Then he addressed the meeting on Temperance, his audience consisting chiefly of adults. But, in the very front seat, the same earnest frowning boy fixed him with a determined gaze. When the Bishop first encountered this gaze he became slightly disconcerted, and lost his place in his notes. Then he tried to forget the disturbing presence and address his remarks to the middle of the hall. But there was something hypnotic in the small boy's gaze. In the end the Bishop yielded to it. He fixed his eyes obediently upon William. He harangued William earnestly and forcibly upon the necessity of self-control and the effect of alcohol upon the liver. And William returned his gaze unblinkingly.

After the meeting William wandered down the road to the Vicarage. He pondered gloomily over his wasted afternoon. Fate had not thrown the Bishop's handkerchief in his path. But he did not yet despair.

On the way he met Ginger. Ginger drew out his interminable coloured handkerchief and shook it proudly.

'D'ye mean to *say*,' he said to William, 'that you still use those old *white* ones?'

William looked at him with cold scorn.

'I'm too busy to bother with you jus' now,' he said.

Ginger went on.

William looked cautiously through the Vicarage hedge. Nothing was to be seen. He crawled inside the garden and round to the back of the house, which was invisible from the road. The Bishop was tired after his address. He lay outstretched upon a deckchair beneath a tree.

Over the head and face of His Lordship was stretched a large superfine linen handkerchief. William's set stern expression brightened. On hands and knees he began to crawl through the grass towards the portly form, his tongue protruding from his pursed lips.

Crouching behind the chair, he braced himself for the crime; he measured the distance between the chair and the garden gate.

One, two, three – then suddenly the portly form stirred, the handkerchief was firmly withdrawn by a podgy hand, and a dignified voice yawned and said: 'Heigh-ho!'

At the same moment the Bishop sat up. William, from his refuge behind the chair, looked wildly round. The door of the house was opening. There was only one thing to do. William was as nimble as a monkey. Like a flash of lightning he disappeared up the tree. It was a very leafy tree. It completely concealed William, but William had a good bird's-eye view of the world beneath him. The Vicar came out rubbing his hands.

'You rested, My Lord?' he said.

'I'm afraid I've had forty winks,' said His Lordship pleasantly. 'Just dropped off, you know. I dreamt about that boy who was at the meeting this afternoon.'

'What boy, My Lord?' asked the Vicar.

'I noticed him at the Sale of Work and the meeting – he looked – he looked a soulful boy. I daresay you know him.'

The Vicar considered.

'I can't think of any boy round here like that,' he said.

The Bishop sighed.

'He may have been a stranger, of course,' he said meditatively. 'It seemed an earnest *questing* face – as if the boy wanted something – *needed* something. I hope my little talk helped him.'

'Without doubt it did, My Lord,' said the Vicar politely. 'I thought we might dine out here – the days draw out so pleasantly now.'

Up in his tree, William with smirks and hand-rubbing and mincing (though soundless) movements of his lips kept up a running imitation of the Vicar's speech, for the edification apparently of a caterpillar that was watching him intently.

The Vicar went in to order dinner in the garden. The

Bishop drew the delicate handkerchief once more over his rubicund features. In the tree William abandoned his airy pastime, and his face took on again the expression of soulful earnestness that had pleased the Bishop.

The breast of the Bishop on the lawn began to rise and sink. The figure of the Vicar was visible at the study window as he gazed with fond pride upon the slumbers of his distinguished guest. William dared not descend in view of that watching figure. Finally it sat down in a chair by the window and began to read a book.

Then William began to act. He took from his pocket a bent pin attached to a piece of string. This apparatus lived permanently in his pocket, because he had not given up hope of catching a trout in the village stream. He lowered this cautiously and drew the bent pin carefully on to the white linen expanse.

It caught – joy!

'Phut!' said the Bishop, bringing down his hand heavily, not on the pin, but near it.

The pin was loosened – William drew it back cautiously up into the tree, and the Bishop settled himself once more to his slumbers.

Again the pin descended – again it caught.

'Phut!' said the Bishop, testily shaking the handkerchief, and again loosening the pin.

Leaning down from his leafy retreat William made one last desperate effort. He drew the bent pin sharply across. It missed the handkerchief and it caught the Bishop's ear. The Bishop sat up with a scream. William, pin and string, withdrew into the shade of the branches. 'Crumbs!' said William desperately to the caterpillar, 'talk about bad *luck*!'

The Vicar ran out from the house, full of concern at the sound of the Bishop's scream.

FROM THE TREE WILLIAM MADE A LAST DESPERATE EFFORT.

'I've been badly stung in the ear by some insect,' said the Bishop in a voice that was pained and dignified. 'Some virulent tropical insect, I should think – very painful. Very painful indeed—'

'My Lord,' said the Vicar, 'I am so sorry – so very

12

sorry – a thousand pardons – can I procure some remedy for you – vaseline, ammonia – er – cold cream—?' Up in the tree the pantomimic imitation of him went on much to William's satisfaction.

'No, no, no, no,' snapped the Bishop. 'This must be a bad place for insects, that's all. Even before that some heavy creatures came banging against my handkerchief. I put my handkerchief over my face for protection. If I had failed to do that I should have been badly stung.'

THE BENT PIN CAUGHT THE BISHOP'S EAR, AND THE BISHOP SAT UP WITH A LITTLE SCREAM.

'Shall we dine indoors, then, My Lord?' said the Vicar.

'Oh, no, no, NO!' said the Bishop impatiently.

The Vicar sat down upon his chair. William collected

a handful of acorns and began to drop them one by one upon the Vicar's bald head. He did this simply because he could not help it. The sight of the Vicar's bald head was irresistible. Each time an acorn struck the Vicar's bald head it bounced up into the air, and the Vicar put up his hand and rubbed his head. At first he tried to continue his conversation on the state of the parish finances with the Bishop but his replies became distrait and incoherent. He moved his chair slightly. William moved the position of his arm and continued to drop acorns.

At last the Bishop noticed it.

'The acorns seem to be falling,' he said.

The Vicar rubbed his head again.

'Don't they?' he said.

'Rather early,' commented the Bishop.

'Isn't it?' he said as another acorn bounced upon his head.

The Bishop began to take quite an interest in the unusual phenomenon.

'I shouldn't be surprised if there was some sort of blight in that tree,' he said. 'It would account for the premature dropping of the acorns and for the insects that attacked me.'

'Exactly,' said the Vicar irritably, as yet another acorn hit him. William's aim was unerring.

Here a diversion was caused by the maid who came out to lay the table. They watched her in silence. The Vicar moved his chair again, and William, after pocketing his friend the caterpillar, shifted his position in the tree again to get a better aim.

'Do you know,' said the Bishop, 'I believe that there is a cat in the tree. Several times I have heard a slight rustling.'

It would have been better for William to remain silent, but William's genius occasionally misled him. He was anxious to prevent investigation; to prove once and for all his identity as a cat.

He leant forward and uttered a re-echoing 'Mi-*aw-aw-aw*!'

As imitations go it was rather good.

There was a slight silence. Then:

'It *is* a cat,' said the Bishop in triumph.

'Excuse me, My Lord,' said the Vicar.

He went softly into the house and returned holding a shoe.

'This will settle His Feline Majesty,' he smiled.

Then he hurled the shoe violently into the tree.

'Shh! Scoot!' he said as he did it.

William was annoyed. The shoe narrowly missed his face. He secured it and waited.

15

'I hope you haven't lost the shoe,' said the Bishop anxiously.

'Oh, no. The gardener's boy or someone will get it for me. It's the best thing to do with cats. It's probably scared it on to the roof.'

He settled himself in his chair comfortably with a smile.

William leant down, held the shoe deliberately over the bald head, then dropped it.

'Damn!' said the Vicar. 'Excuse me, My Lord.'

'H'm,' said the Bishop. 'Er – yes – most annoying. It lodged in a branch for a time probably, and then obeyed the force of gravity.'

The Vicar was rubbing his head. William wanted to enjoy the sight of the Vicar rubbing his head. He moved a little further up the branch. He forgot all caution. He forgot that the branch on which he was was not a very secure branch, and that the further up he moved the less secure it became.

There was the sound of a rending and a crashing, and on to the table between the amazed Vicar and Bishop descended William's branch and William.

The Bishop gazed at him. 'Why, that's the boy,' he said.

William sat up among the debris of broken glasses and crockery. He discovered that he was bruised and that his

16

hand was cut by one of the broken glasses. He extricated himself from the branch and the table, and stood rubbing his bruises and sucking his hand.

'Crumbs!' was all he said.

The Vicar was gazing at him speechlessly.

'You know, my boy,' said the Bishop in mild reproach, 'that's a very curious thing to do – to hide up there for the purpose of eavesdropping. I know that you are an earnest, well-meaning little boy, and that you were interested in my address this afternoon, and I daresay you were hoping to listen to me again, but this is my time for relaxation, you know. Suppose the Vicar and I had been talking about something we didn't want you to hear? I'm sure you wouldn't like to listen to things people didn't want you to hear, would you?'

William stared at him in unconcealed amazement. The Vicar, with growing memories of acorns and shoes and 'damns' and with murder in his heart, was picking up twigs and broken glass. He knew that he could not, in the Bishop's presence, say the things to William and do the things to William that he wanted to do and say. He contented himself with saying:

'You'd better go home now. Tell your father I'll be coming to see him tomorrow.'

'A well-meaning, little boy, I'm sure,' said the Bishop

kindly. 'Well-meaning, but unwise – er – unwise. But your attentiveness during the meeting did you credit, my boy – did you credit.'

William, for all his ingenuity, could think of no remark suitable to the occasion.

'Hurry up,' said the Vicar.

William turned to go. He knew when he was beaten. He had spent a lot of time and trouble and had not even secured the episcopal handkerchief. He had bruised himself and cut himself. He understood the Vicar's veiled threat. He saw his already distant chances of pocket-money vanish into nothingness when the cost of the Vicar's glasses and plates was added to the landing window. He wouldn't have minded if he'd got the handkerchief. He wouldn't have minded anything if—

'Don't suck your hand, my boy,' said the Bishop. 'An open cut like that is most dangerous. Poison works into the system by it. You remember I told you how the poison of alcohol works into the system – well, any kind of poison can work into it by a cut – don't suck it; keep it covered up – haven't you a handkerchief? – here, take mine. You needn't trouble to return it. It's an old one.'

The Bishop was deeply touched by what he called the 'bright spirituality' of the smile with which William thanked him.

18

*

William, limping slightly, his hand covered by a grimy rag, came out into the garden, drawing from his pocket with a triumphant flourish an enormous violently-coloured silk handkerchief. Robert, who was weeding the rose-bed, looked up. 'Here,' he called, 'you can jolly well go and put that handkerchief of mine back.'

William continued his limping but proud advance.

''S' all right,' he called airily, 'the Bishop's is on your dressing-table.'

Robert dropped the trowel.

'Gosh!' he gasped, and hastened indoors to investigate.

William went down to the gate, smiling very slightly to himself.

'The days are drawing out so pleasantly,' he was saying to himself in a mincing accent. 'Vaseline – ammonia – er – or cold cream— Damn!'

He leant over the gate, took out his caterpillar, satisfied himself that it was still alive, put it back and looked up and down the road. In the distance he caught sight of the figure of his friend.

'Gin – *ger*,' he yelled in hideous shrillness.

He waved his coloured handkerchief carelessly in greeting as he called. Then he swaggered out into the road . . .

CHAPTER 2

HENRI LEARNS THE LANGUAGE

It was Joan who drew William and the Outlaws from their immemorial practice of playing at Pirates and Red Indians.

'I'm tired of being a squaw,' she said plaintively, 'an' I'm tired of walking the plank an' I want to be something else an' do something else.'

Joan was the only girl whose existence the Outlaws officially recognised. This was partly owing to Joan's own personal attractiveness and partly to the fact that an admiration for Joan was the only human weakness of their manly leader, William. Thus Joan was admitted to all such games as required the female element. The others she was graciously allowed to watch.

They received her outburst with pained astonishment.

'Well,' said Ginger coldly, 'wot else is there to do an' be?'

Ginger felt that the very foundation of the Society of Outlaws was being threatened. The Outlaws had played at Pirates and Red Indians since their foundation.

'Let's play at being ordinary people,' said Joan.

'Ordinary people—!' exploded Douglas. 'There's no *playin'* in bein' *ordinary* people. Wot's the good—?'

'Let's be Jasmine Villas,' said Joan, warming to her theme. 'We'll each be a person in Jasmine Villas—'

William, who had so far preserved a judicial silence, now said:

'I don' mind playin' ornery people s'long as we don' do ornery things.'

'Oh, no, William,' said Joan with the air of meekness with which she always received William's oracles, 'we needn't do ornery things.'

'Then bags me be ole Mr Burwash.'

'And me Miss Milton next door,' said Joan hastily.

The Outlaws were beginning to see vague possibilities in the game.

'An' me Mr Luton,' said Ginger.

'An' me Mr Buck,' said Douglas.

Henry, the remaining outlaw, looked around him indignantly. Jasmine Villas only contained four houses.

'An' wot about *me*?' he said.

'Oh, you be a policeman wot walks about outside,' said William.

Henry, mollified, began to practise a commanding strut.

In the field behind the old barn that was the scene of most of their activities they began to construct Jasmine Villas by boundary lines of twigs. Each inhabitant took up their position inside a twig-encircled enclosure, and Henry paraded officiously around.

'Now we'll jus' have a minute to think of what things to do,' said William, 'an' then I'll begin.'

William was sitting in his back garden thinking out exploits to perform that afternoon in the character of Mr Burwash. The game of Jasmine Villas was 'taken on' beyond all expectation. Mr Burwash stole Miss Milton's washing during her afternoon siesta, Mr Buck locked up Mr Luton in his coal cellar and ate up all his provisions, and always the entire population of Jasmine Villas was chased round the field by Henry, the policeman, several times during a game. Often some of them were arrested, tried, condemned and imprisoned by the stalwart Henry, to be rescued later by a joint force of the other inhabitants of Jasmine Villas.

William, sitting on an inverted flower pot, absent-mindedly chewing grass and throwing sticks for his mongrel, Jumble, to worry, was wondering whether (in his role of Mr Burwash) it would be more exciting to go mad and resist the ubiquitous Henry's efforts to take him to an asylum, or marry Miss Milton. The only drawback to the latter plan was that they had provided no clergyman. However, perhaps a policeman would do . . . Finally he decided that it would be more exciting to go mad and leave Miss Milton to someone else.

''Ello!'

A thin, lugubrious face appeared over the fence that separated William's garden from the next door garden.

''Ello!' replied William, throwing it a cold glance and returning to his pastime of entertaining Jumble.

'I weesh to leearn ze Eengleesh,' went on the owner of the lugubrious face. 'My godmother 'ere she talk ze correct Eengleesh. It ees ze idiomatic Eengleesh I weesh to leearn – how you call it? – ze slang. You talk ze slang – ees it not?'

William gave the intruder a devastating glare, gathering up his twigs and with a commanding 'Hi, Jumble', set off round the side of the house.

'Oh, William!'

William sighed as he recognised his mother's voice. This was followed by his mother's head which appeared at the opening drawing-room window.

'I'm busy *jus'* now –' said William sternly.

'William, Mrs Frame next door has a godson staying with her and he is so anxious to mix with boys and learn

23

colloquial English. I've asked him to tea this afternoon. Oh, here he is.'

The owner of the thin lugubrious face – a young man of about eighteen – appeared behind William.

'I made a way – 'ow say you? – through a 'ole in ze fence. I weeshed to talk wiz ze boy.'

'Well, now, William,' said Mrs Brown persuasively, 'you might spend the afternoon with Henri and talk to him.'

William's face was a study in horror and indignation.

'I shan't know what to say to him,' he said desperately. 'I can't talk his kind of talk.'

'I'm sure that'll be quite all right,' said Mrs Brown, kindly. 'He speaks English very well. Just talk to him simply and naturally.'

She brought the argument to an end by closing the window and leaving an embittered William to undertake his new responsibility.

''Ave you a 'oliday zis afternoon,' began his new responsibility.

'I 'ave,' said William simply and naturally.

'Zen we weel talk,' said Henri with enthusiasm. 'We weel talk an' you weel teach to me ze slang.'

''Fraid I've gotter play a game this afternoon,' said William icily, as they set off down the road.

'I weel play,' said Henri pleasantly, 'I like ze games.'

'I'm 'fraid,' said William with equal pleasantness, 'there won't be no room for you.'

'I weel watch zen,' said Henri, 'I like too ze watching.'

Henri, who had spent the afternoon watching the game, was on his way home. He had enjoyed watching the game. He had watched a realistically insane Mr Burwash resist all attempts at capture on the part of the local policeman. He had watched Mr Luton propose to Miss Milton, and he had watched Mr Buck in his end house being gloriously and realistically drunk. This was an accomplishment of Douglas's that was forbidden at home under threat of severe punishment, but it was greatly appreciated by the Outlaws.

Henri walked along jauntily, practising slang to himself.

'Oh, ze Crumbs . . . oh, ze Crikey . . . ze jolly well . . . righto . . . git out . . . ze bash on ze mug . . .'

General Moult – fat and important-looking – came breezily down the road.

'Ah, Henri . . . how are you getting on?'

'Ze jolly well,' said Henri.

'Been for a walk?' said the General yet more breezily.

'Non . . . I been to Jasmine Villas . . . Oh, ze Crumbs . . .

I see ole Meester Burwash go – 'ow you say it? – off ze head – out of ze chump.'

'*What?*'

'Oh, yes,' said Henri, 'an' the policeman 'e come an' try to take 'im away an' 'e fight an' fight, an' ze policeman 'e go for 'elp—'

The General's mouth was hanging open in amazement.

'B-but, are you *sure?*' he gasped.

'Oh, yes,' said Henri cheerfully. 'I 'ave *been* zere, I 'ave ze jolly well watch eet.'

'But, good heavens!' said the General, and hastened in the direction of Jasmine Villas.

Henri sauntered on by himself.

'Ze 'oly aunt . . . a'right . . . ze booze . . .' he murmured softly.

At the corner of the road he ran into Mr Graham Graham. Mr Graham Graham was tall and lank, with pince-nez and an earnest expression. Mr Graham Graham's earnest expression did not belie his character. He was, among other things, the President of the local Temperance Society. He had met Henri with his godmother the day before.

'Well, Henri,' he said earnestly. 'And how have you been spending your time?'

'I 'ave been to Jasmine Villas,' said Henri.

'Ah, yes – to whom—?'

Henri interrupted.

'An' I 'ave seen Meester Buck . . . oh, ze crumbs . . . 'ow say you? . . . tight . . . boozed . . . derrunk.'

Mr Graham Graham paled.

'Never!' he said.

Mr Buck was the Secretary of the local Temperance Society.

'Oh, yes, ze 'oly aunt!' said Henri, 'ze policeman 'e 'elp 'im into the 'ouse – 'e was, 'ow say you? Ro-o-o-o-olling.'

'This is impossible,' said Mr Graham Graham sternly.

'I 'ave seed it,' said Henri simply. 'I laugh . . . oh, ze Crikey . . . *'ow* I laugh . . .'

Mr Graham Graham turned upon Henri a cold condemning silent glance then set off in the direction of Jasmine Villas.

Henri wandered homewards.

He met his godmother coming out of her front gate.

'We're going to Mrs Brown's to tea, you know, Henri,' she reminded him.

'A'right,' said Henri. 'A'right – righto.'

He accompanied her to Mrs Brown's.

'And did you spend the afternoon with William?' said Mrs Brown pleasantly.

'Oh, yes,' said Henri as he sat down comfortably by

the fire, 'at ze Jasmine Villas . . . Mr Luton e' kees Miss Milton in the garden.'

Henri's godmother dropped her buttered scone.

'*Nonsense!*' she said.

''E did,' said Henri calmly. 'I 'ave seed 'im. An' she gave 'im – 'ow say you? – ze bash on ze mug. But she tell me she goin' to marry 'im – righto.'

'She *told* you?' gasped Mrs Brown.

'Oh, yes,' said Henri, 'she tell me so 'erself.'

Both Mrs Brown and Henri's godmother were pale.

'Do you think she doesn't know that he's married and separated from his wife?' said Henri's godmother.

'I don't know,' said Mrs Brown. 'I feel that I can't eat a thing now. Someone ought to tell her at once.'

'Let's go,' said Henri's godmother suddenly, 'before she tells anyone else. The poor woman!'

They went out quickly, leaving Henri alone in the drawing-room. Henri chose a large sugared cake and began to munch it.

'Ze jolly well good,' he commented contentedly.

The General approached Mr Burwash's house cautiously. There was no sign of a disturbance. Evidently the policeman had not yet returned with help. The General entered the garden and went on tiptoe to the morning-

room window. He was full of curiosity. There was the
madman. He was sitting at a table with his back to the
window. There was a mad look about his very back. The
General was suddenly inspired by the idea of making
the capture single-handed. It would be a glorious page
in the annals of the village. The front door was open.
The General entered and walked very slowly down the
hall. The morning-room door was open. It was here that
the General made the painful discovery that his boots
squeaked. The squeaking would undoubtedly attract the
attention of the lunatic as he entered. The General had
another inspiration. He dropped down upon his hands
and knees. He could thus make his way unseen and
unheard to the back of the madman, then spring to his
feet and overpower him.

He entered the room.

He reached the middle of the room.

Then Mr Burwash turned round.

Mr Burwash was met by the sight of the General
creeping gingerly and delicately across his morning-room
carpet on hands and knees. Mr Burwash leapt to the not
unreasonable conclusion that the General had gone mad.
Mr Burwash knew that a madman must be humoured.
He also dropped upon his hands and knees.

'Bow-wow!' he said.

If the General thought he was a dog, the General must be humoured.

'Bow-wow!' promptly replied the General.

The General also knew that madmen must be humoured.

They continued this conversation for several minutes.

Then Mr Burwash, intent on escape, made a leap towards the door, and the General, intent on capture, made a leap to intercept him.

They leapt about the room excitedly uttering short, shrill barks. The General never quite knew what made him change into a cat. It was partly that he was tired of barking and partly that he hoped to lure Mr Burwash after him into the more open space of the hall and there overpower him. Mr Burwash's pursuit was realistic, and the General, violently chased into the hall, decided to leave the capture to the police after all, and made for the hall door. But a furiously barking Mr Burwash cut off his retreat. The General, still miaowing unconsciously in a high treble voice, scampered on all fours up the stairs and took refuge in a small room at the top, slamming the door against the pursuing lunatic. They key was turned in the lock from outside.

At the top of the stairs Mr Burwash stood trembling slightly, and wiped his brow. A violent sound of kicking came from the locked room.

*

Mrs Brown and Henri's godmother heard vaguely the distant sounds of the kicking next door, but their delicate interview with Miss Milton was taking all their attention.

Miss Milton, who had been to see a girl whom she was engaging as housemaid for Mr Luton, was just taking off her things. Miss Milton kept a purely maternal eye upon Mr Luton.

'You know, dear,' said Henri's godmother, 'we felt we had to come and tell you as soon as we heard the news. He's got one already.'

'Who?' said Miss Milton, angular and severe-looking.

'Mr Luton.'

'He might have told me,' said Miss Milton.

'But she's left him,' put in Mrs Brown.

'Then I'd better see about providing him with another,' said Miss Milton.

'She – she's not divorced,' gasped Mrs Brown.

'I should hope not,' said Miss Milton primly. 'I'm always most particular about that sort of thing.'

'But when we heard he'd been seen kissing you—' said Henri's mother.

Miss Milton gave a piercing scream.

'ME?' she said.

'Yes, when we heard that Mr Luton had been seen—'

31

Miss Milton gave a still more piercing scream.

'Slanderers,' she shrieked, 'vampires . . .'

She advanced upon them quivering with rage.

'I'm so sorry,' gasped Mrs Brown retreating precipitately. 'Quite a mistake . . . a misunderstanding . . .'

'Liars . . . hypocrites . . . snakes in the grass!' screamed Miss Milton, still advancing.

Mrs Brown and Henri's godmother fled trembling to the road. Miss Milton's screams still rent the air. There, two curious sights met their eyes. The General and Mr Graham Graham were making their exits from the two end houses in unconventional fashion. Mr Graham Graham fell down the steps and rolled down the garden path to the road. An infuriated Mr Buck watched his departure.

'I'll teach you to come and insult respectable people,' shouted Mr Buck. 'Drunkard indeed! And I've been Secretary of the Temperance Society for forty years. You're drunk, let me tell you—'

Mr Graham Graham, still sitting in the road, put on his hat.

'I'm not drunk,' he said with dignity.

'I'll have the law on you,' shouted Mr Buck. 'It's libel, that's what it is—'

Mr Graham Graham gathered his collar ends and tried to find his stud.

'I merely repeat what I've heard,' he said.

Mr Buck slammed the door and Mr Graham Graham staggered to his feet.

Then he stood open-mouthed, his eyes fixed on the other end house. The stout figure of the General could be seen emerging from a small first-floor window and making a slow and ungraceful descent down a drainpipe. It was noticed that he had no hat and that his knees were very dusty. Once on the ground he ran wildly across the garden into the road, almost charging the little group who were watching him. With pale, horror-struck faces the four of them gazed at each other.

'Henri told me—' all four began simultaneously, then stopped.

'D-do come and have some tea,' said Mrs Brown hysterically.

William was leading his Outlaws quietly round from the front gate to the back of the house, passing the drawing-room window on tiptoe. Suddenly William stopped dead, gazing with interest into the drawing-room. The expected tea party was not there. Only Henri, still eating sugar cakes, was there. William put his head through the open window.

'I say,' he said in a hoarse whisper, 'they been an' gone?'

'Oh, yes,' smiled Henri, 'they been an' gone – righto.'

'Come on!' said William to his followers.

They crept into the hall and then guiltily into the drawing-room. William looked at the plates of dainty food with widening eyes.

'Shu'ly,' he remarked plaintively, ''f they've been an' gone they can't mind us jus' finishin' up what they've left. *Shu'ly.*'

William made this statement less at the dictates of truth than at the dictates of an empty stomach.

'Jus' – jus' look out of the window, Ongry,' he said, 'an' tell us if anyone comes.'

Henri obligingly took up his position at the window and the Outlaws gave themselves up wholeheartedly to the task of 'finishing up'.

They finished up the buttered scones and they finished up the bread and butter and they finished up the sandwiches and they finished up the biscuits and they finished up the small cakes and they finished up the two large cakes.

'I'm jus' a bit tired of this ole Jasmine Villas game,' said William, his mouth full of sugar cake. 'I votes we go back to Pirates an' Red Injuns tomorrow.'

The Outlaws, who were still busy, agreed with grunts.

'I think—' began Douglas, but just then Henri at the window ejaculated shrilly, 'Oh, ze 'oly aunt.'

The Outlaws hastily joined him. Four people were coming down the road. The General – *could* it be the General (the drain pipe had been very dirty)? – Mr Graham Graham, his collar open, his tie awry, Henri's godmother with her hat on one side, and Mrs Brown, her usual look of placid equanimity replaced by a look that was almost wild. They were certainly coming to the Browns' house, William looked guiltily at the empty plates and cakestand. Except upon the carpet (for the Outlaws were not born drawing-room eaters) there was not a crumb to be seen.

'P'raps,' said William hastily to his friends, 'p'raps we'd better go now.'

His friends agreed.

They went as quietly and unostentatiously as possible by way of the back regions.

Henri remained at the window. He watched the curious quartette as they came in at the gate.

Details of their appearance, unnoticed before, became clear as they drew nearer. 'Ze Crumbs *an'* ze Crikey!' ejaculated Henri.

It was two hours later. William sat disconsolately upon the upturned plant pot throwing stones half-heartedly at the fence. Jumble sat disconsolately by him snapping

AT THE WINDOW HENRI EXCLAIMED SHRILLY, 'OH, ZE
'OLY AUNT!' AND THE OUTLAWS HASTILY JOINED HIM.

half-heartedly at flies. The Outlaws had nobly shared the sugar cakes with Jumble and he was just beginning to wish that they hadn't . . .

Suddenly Henri's face appeared at the top of the fence.

''Ello!' he said.

''Ello!' sighed William.

'Zey talk to me,' said Henri sadly, ''*ow* zey talk to me jus' because I tell 'em about your leetle game.'

FOUR PEOPLE WERE COMING DOWN THE ROAD –
FOUR VERY ANGRY PEOPLE.

'Yes,' said William bitterly, 'and *'ow* they talk to me jus' 'cause we finished up a few ole cakes and things left over from tea. You'd think to hear 'em that they'd have been glad to come home and find me starved dead.'

Henri leant yet further over the fence.

'But zey looked . . . *'ow* zey looked!'

There was silence for a moment while the mental vision of ''ow zey looked' came to both. Then William's rare laugh – unmusical and penetrating – rang out. Mrs Brown, who was suffering from a severe headache as the result of the events of the afternoon, hastily closed the drawing-room window. Followed Henri's laugh – high-pitched and like the neighing of a horse. Henri's godmother tore herself with a groan from the bed on which she was indulging in a nervous breakdown and flung up her bedroom window.

'Henri, are you ill?' she cried. 'What is it?'

'Oh, ze nosings,' replied Henri.

Then, leaning yet more dangerously over the fence, 'What ze game you goin' to play tomorrow, Willem?'

'Pirates,' said William, regaining his usual calm. 'Like to come?'

'Oh, ze jolly well righto yes!' said Henri.

CHAPTER 3

THE SWEET LITTLE GIRL IN WHITE

The Hall stood empty most of the year, but occasionally tenants re-awoke the passing interest of the village in it. This summer it was taken by a Mr and Mrs Bott with their daughter. Mr Bott's name decorated most of the hoardings of his native country. On these hoardings citizens of England were urged to safeguard their digestion by taking Bott's Sauce with their meat. After reading Bott's advertisements one felt convinced that any food without Bott's Sauce was rank poison. One even felt that it would be safer to live on Bott's Sauce alone. On such feelings had Mr Bott – as rubicund and rotund as one of his own bottles of sauce – reared a fortune sufficient to enable him to take the Hall for the summer without, as the saying is, turning a hair.

William happened to be sitting on the fence by the side of the road when the motor containing Mr and Mrs Bott – both stout and overdressed – and Miss Violet Elizabeth Bott and Miss Violet Elizabeth Bott's nurse flashed by. William was not interested. He was at the moment engaged in whittling a stick and watching the antics of his mongrel, Jumble, as he caught and worried each shaving. But he had a glimpse of a small child with an elaborately curled head and an elaborately flounced white dress sitting by an elaborately uniformed nurse. He gazed after the equipage scowling.

'Huh!' he said, and it is impossible to convey in print the scorn of that monosyllable as uttered by William. '*A girl!*'

Then he returned to his whittling.

William's mother met Mrs Bott at the Vicar's. Mrs Bott, who always found strangers more sympathetic than people who knew her well, confided her troubles to Mrs Brown. Her troubles included her own rheumatism, Mr Bott's liver, and the carelessness of Violet Elizabeth's nurse.

'Always reading these here novelettes, the girl is. I hope you'll come and see me, dear, and didn't someone say you had a little boy? Do bring him. I want Violet Elizabeth to get to know some nice little children.'

Mrs Brown hesitated. She was aware that none of her acquaintances would have described William as a nice little child. Mrs Bott misunderstood her hesitation. She laid a fat-ringed hand on her knee.

'I know, dear. You're careful who the little laddie knows, like me. Well now, you needn't worry. I've brought up our Violet Elizabeth most particular. She's a girlie who wouldn't do your little boysie any harm—'

'Oh,' gasped Mrs Brown, 'it's not that.'

'Then you'll come, dearie, and bring the little boysie with you, won't you?'

She took Mrs Brown's speechlessness for consent.

'*Me?*' said William indignantly. 'Me go to tea with that ole girl? *Me?*'

'She – she's a nice little girl,' said Mrs Brown weakly.

'I saw her,' said William scathingly, 'curls and things.'

'Well, you must come. She's expecting you.'

'I only hope,' said William sternly, 'that she won't 'spect me to *talk* to her.'

'She'll expect you to *play* with her, I'm sure,' said his mother.

'Play!' said William. '*Play?* With a girl? *Me?* Huh!'

William, pale and proud, and dressed in his best suit, his heart steeled to his humiliating fate, went with his mother to the Hall the next week. He was silent all the way there. His thoughts were too deep for words. Mrs Brown watched him anxiously.

41

An over-dressed Mrs Bott was sitting in an over-furnished drawing-room. She rose at once with an over-effusive smile and held out over-ringed hands.

'So you've brought dear little boysie,' she began.

The over-effusive smile died away before the look that William turned on her.

'Er – I hadn't thought of him quite like that,' she said weakly, 'but I'm sure he's sweet,' she added hastily.

William greeted her coldly and politely, then took his seat and sat like a small statue scowling in front of him. His hair had been brushed back with so much vigour and application of liquid that it looked as if it were painted on his head.

'Would you like to look at a picture book, boysie?' she said.

William did not answer. He merely looked at her and she hastily turned away to talk to Mrs Brown. She talked about her rheumatism and Mr Bott's liver and the incompetence of Violet Elizabeth's nurse.

Then Violet Elizabeth entered. Violet Elizabeth's fair hair was not naturally curly but as the result of great daily labour on the part of the much maligned nurse it stood up in a halo of curls round her small head. The curls looked almost, if not quite, natural. Violet Elizabeth's small pink and white face shone with cleanliness. Violet Elizabeth was so treasured and guarded and surrounded with every care that her small pink and white face had never been known to do anything else except shine with cleanliness. But the pièce de résistance about Violet Elizabeth's appearance was her skirts. Violet Elizabeth was dressed in a white lace-trimmed dress with a blue waistband and beneath the miniature blue waistband, her skirts stood out like a tiny ballet dancer's in a filmy froth of lace-trimmed petticoats. From this cascade emerged Violet Elizabeth's bare legs, to disappear ultimately into white silk socks and white buckskin shoes.

William gazed at this engaging apparition in horror.

'Good afternoon,' said Violet Elizabeth primly.

'Good afternoon,' said William in a hollow voice.

'Take the little boysie into the garden, Violet Elizabeth,' said her mother, 'and play with him nicely.'

William and Violet Elizabeth eyed each other apprehensively.

'Come along, boy,' said Violet Elizabeth at last, holding out a hand.

William ignored the hand and with the air of a hero bound to his execution, accompanied Violet Elizabeth into the garden.

Mrs Brown's eyes followed them anxiously.

*

'Whath your name?' said Violet Elizabeth.

She lisped! She would, thought William bitterly, with those curls and those skirts. She would. He felt at any rate relieved that none of his friends could see him in the unmanly situation – talking to a kid like that – all eyes and curls and skirts.

'William Brown,' he said, distantly, looking over her head as if he did not see her.

'How old are you?'

'Eleven.'

'My nameth Violet Elizabeth.'

He received the information in silence.

'I'm thix.'

He made no comment. He examined the distant view with an abstracted frown.

'Now you muth play with me.'

William allowed his cold glance to rest upon her.

'I don't play little girls' games,' he said scathingly. But Violet Elizabeth did not appear to be scathed.

'Don' you know any little girlth?' she said pityingly. 'I'll teach you little girlth gameth,' she added pleasantly.

'I don't *want* to,' said William. 'I don't *like* them. I don't *like* little girls' games. I don't want to know 'em.'

Violet Elizabeth gazed at him open-mouthed.

'Don't you *like* little girlth?' she said.

'*Me?*' said William with superior dignity. 'Me? I don't know anything about 'em. Don't want to.'

'D-don't you like me?' quavered Violet Elizabeth in incredulous amazement. William looked at her. Her blue eyes filled slowly with tears, her lips quivered.

'I like you,' she said. 'Don't you like me?'

William stared at her in horror.

'You – you *do* like me, don't you?'

William was silent.

A large shining tear welled over and trickled down the small pink cheek.

'You're making me cry,' sobbed Violet Elizabeth. 'You are. You're making me cry, 'cause you won't say you like me.'

'I – I do like you,' said William desperately. 'Honest – I do. Don't cry. I do like you. Honest!'

A smile broke through the tear-stained face.

'I'm tho glad,' she said simply. 'You like all little girlth, don't you?' She smiled at him hopefully. 'You, do don't you?'

William, pirate and Red Indian and desperado, William, woman-hater and girl-despiser, looked round wildly for escape and found none.

Violet Elizabeth's eyes filled with tears again.

45

'You *do* like all little girlth, don't you?' she persisted with quavering lip. 'You do, don't you?'

It was a nightmare to William. They were standing in full view of the drawing-room window. At any moment a grown-up might appear. He would be accused of brutality, of making little Violet Elizabeth cry. And, strangely enough, the sight of Violet Elizabeth with tear-filled eyes and trembling lips made him feel that he must have been brutal indeed. Beneath his horror he felt bewildered.

'Yes, I do,' he said hastily, 'I do. Honest I do.'

She smiled again radiantly through her tears. 'You with you wath a little girl, don't you?'

'Er – yes. Honest I do,' said the unhappy William.

'Kith me,' she said raising her glowing face.

William was broken.

He brushed her cheek with his.

'Thath not a kith,' said Violet Elizabeth.

'It's my kind of a kiss,' said William.

'All right. Now leth play fairieth. I'll thow you how.'

On the way home Mrs Brown, who always hoped vaguely that little girls would have a civilising effect on William, asked William if he had enjoyed it. William had spent most of the afternoon in the character of a gnome attending upon Violet Elizabeth in the character of the Fairy Queen. Any attempt at rebellion had been met with tear-filled eyes and trembling lips. He was feeling embittered with life.

'If all girls are like that—' said William. 'Well, when you think of all the hundreds of girls there must be in the world – well, it makes you feel sick.'

Never had liberty and the comradeship of his own sex seemed sweeter to William than it did the next day when he set off whistling carelessly, his hands in his pockets, Jumble at his heels, to meet Ginger and Douglas across the fields.

'You didn't come yesterday,' they said when they met. They had missed William, the leader.

'No,' he said shortly, 'went out to tea.'

'Where?' they said with interest.

'Nowhere in particular,' said William inaccurately.

A feeling of horror overcame him at the memory. If they knew – if they'd seen . . . He blushed with shame at the very thought. To regain his self-respect he punched Ginger and knocked off Douglas's cap. After the slight scuffle that ensued they set off down the road.

'What'll we do this morning?' said Ginger.

It was sunny. It was holiday time. They had each other and a dog. Boyhood could not wish for more. The whole world lay before them.

'Let's go trespassin',' said William the lawless.

'Where?' enquired Douglas.

'Hall woods – and take Jumble.'

'That ole keeper said he'd tell our fathers if he caught us in again,' said Ginger.

'Lettim!' said William, with a dare-devil air, slashing at the hedge with a stick. He was gradually recovering his self-respect. The nightmare memories of yesterday were growing faint. He flung a stone for the eager Jumble and uttered his shrill unharmonious war-whoop. They entered the woods, William leading. He swaggered along the path. He was William, desperado, and scorner of girls. Yesterday was a dream. It must have been. No mere girl would dare even to speak to him. He had never played at fairies with a girl – he, William the pirate king, the robber chief.

'William!'

He turned, his proud smile frozen in horror.

A small figure was flying along the path behind them – a bare-headed figure with elaborate curls and very short lacy bunchy skirts and bare legs with white shoes and socks.

'William, *darling*! I thaw you from the nurthery window coming along the road and I ethcaped. Nurth wath reading a book and I ethcaped. Oh, William darling, play with me again, *do*. It *wath* so nith yethterday.'

William glared at her speechless. He was glad of the

48

presence of his manly friends, yet horrified as to what revelations this terrible young female might make, disgracing him for ever in their eyes.

'Go away,' he said sternly at last, 'we aren't playing girls' games.'

'We don't like girls,' said Ginger contemptuously.

'William doth,' she said indignantly. 'He thaid he did. He thaid he liked all little girlth. He thaid he withed he wath a little girl. He kithed me an' played fairieth with me.'

A glorious blush of a rich and dark red overspread William's countenance.

'*Oh!*' he ejaculated as if astounded at the depth of her untruthfulness, but it was not convincing.

'Oh, you *did*!' said Violet Elizabeth. Somehow that was convincing. Ginger and Douglas looked at William rather coldly. Even Jumble seemed to look slightly ashamed of him.

'Well, come along,' said Ginger, 'we can't stop here all day talking – to a *girl*.'

'But I want to come with you,' said Violet Elizabeth. 'I want to play with you.'

'We're going to play boys' games. You wouldn't like it,' said Douglas who was somewhat of a diplomatist.

'I *like* boyth gameth,' pleaded Violet Elizabeth, and her blue eyes filled with tears, '*pleath* let me come.'

'All right,' said William. 'We can't stop you comin'. Don't take any notice of her,' he said to the others. 'She'll soon get tired of it.'

They set off. William, for the moment abashed and deflated, followed humbly in their wake.

In a low-lying part of the wood was a bog. The bog was always there but as it had rained in the night the bog today was particularly boggy. It was quite possible to skirt this bog by walking round it on the higher ground, but William and his friends never did this. They preferred to pretend that the bog surrounded them on all sides as far as human eye could see and that at one false step they might sink deep in the morass never to be seen again.

'Come along,' called William who had recovered his spirits and position of leadership. 'Come along, my brave fellows . . . tread careful or instant death will be your fate, and don't take any notice of her, she'll soon have had enough.'

For Violet Elizabeth was trotting gaily behind the gallant band.

They did not turn round or look at her, but they could not help seeing her out of the corners of their eyes. She plunged into the bog with a squeal of delight and stamped her elegant white-clad feet into the black mud.

'Ithn't it lovely?' she squealed. 'Dothn't it feel nith – all thquithy between your toth – ithn't it *lovely*? I *like* boyth gameth.'

They could not help looking at her when they emerged. As fairy-like as ever above, her feet were covered with black mud up to above her socks. Shoes and socks were sodden.

'Ith a *lovely* feeling!' she commented delightedly on the other side. 'Leth do it again.'

But William and his band remembered their manly dignity and strode on without answering. She followed with short dancing steps. Each of them carried a stick with which they smote the air or any shrub they passed. Violet Elizabeth secured a stick and faithfully imitated them. They came to a clear space in the wood, occupied chiefly by giant blackberry bushes laden with fat ripe berries.

'Now, my brave fellows,' said William, 'take your fill. 'Tis well we have found this bit of food or we would e'en have starved, an' don' help her or get any for her an' let her get all scratched an' she'll soon have had enough.'

They fell upon the bushes. Violet Elizabeth also fell upon the bushes. She crammed handfuls of ripe blackberries into her mouth. Gradually her pink and white face became obscured beneath a thick covering of blackberry juice stain. Her hands were dark red. Her white dress had lost its whiteness. It was stained and torn. Her bunchy skirts had lost their bunchiness. The brambles tore at her curled hair and drew it into that state of straightness for which Nature had meant it. The brambles scratched her face and arms and legs. And still she ate.

'I'm getting more than any of you,' she cried. 'I geth I'm getting more than any of you. And I'm getting all of a *meth*. Ithn't it *fun*? I like boyth gameth.'

They gazed at her with a certain horrified respect and apprehension. Would they be held responsible for the strange change in her appearance?

They left the blackberry bushes and set off again through the wood. At a sign from William they dropped on all fours and crept cautiously and (as they imagined) silently along the path. Violet Elizabeth dropped also upon her scratched and blackberry stained knees.

'Look at me,' she shrilled proudly. 'I'm doing it too. Juth like boyth.'

'Shh!' William said fiercely.

Violet Elizabeth 'Shh'd' obediently and for a time crawled along contentedly.

'Are we playin' bein' animalth?' she piped at last.

'Shut *up*!' hissed William.

Violet Elizabeth shut up – except to whisper to Ginger who was just in front, 'I'm a thnail – what you?' Ginger did not deign to reply.

At a sign from their leader that all danger was over the Outlaws stood upright. William had stopped.

'We've thrown 'em off the scent,' he said scowling, 'but danger s'rounds us on every side. We'd better plunge into the jungle an' I bet she'll soon've had enough of plungin' into the jungle.'

They left the path and 'plunged' into the dense, shoulder-high undergrowth. At the end of the line 'plunged' Violet Elizabeth. She fought her way determinedly through the bushes. She left remnants of her filmy skirts on nearly every bush. Long spidery arms of brambles caught at her hair again and pulled out her curls. But Violet Elizabeth liked it. 'Ithn't *it fun*?' she piped as she followed.

Under a large tree William stopped.

'Now we'll be Red Indians,' he said, 'an' go huntin'. I'll be Brave Heart same as usual and Ginger be Hawk Face and Douglas be Lightning Eye.'

'An' what shall I be?' said the torn and stained and wild-headed apparition that had been Violet Elizabeth.

Douglas took the matter in hand.

53

'What thall I be?' he mimicked shrilly. 'What thall I be? What thall I be?'

Violet Elizabeth did not run home in tears as he had hoped she would. She laughed gleefully.

'It doth thound funny when you thay it like that!' she said delightedly. 'Oh, it doth! Thay it again! Pleeth thay it again.'

Douglas was nonplussed.

'Anyway,' he said, 'you jolly well aren't going to play, so there.'

'*Pleath* let me play,' said Violet Elizabeth. 'Pleath.'

'No. Go away!'

William and Ginger secretly admired the firm handling of this female by Douglas.

'*Pleath*, Douglath.'

'*No!*'

Violet Elizabeth's blue eyes, fixed pleadingly upon him, filled with tears. Violet Elizabeth's underlip trembled.

'You're making me cry,' she said. A tear traced its course down the blackberry stained cheek.

'*Pleath*, Douglath.'

Douglas hesitated and was lost. 'Oh, well—' he said.

'Oh, thank you, dear Douglath,' said Violet Elizabeth. 'What thall I be?'

'Well,' said William to Douglas sternly. 'Now you've *let* her play I s'pose she'd better be a squaw.'

'A thquaw,' said Violet Elizabeth joyfully, 'what thort of noith doth it make?'

'It's a Indian lady and it doesn't make any sort of a noise,' said Ginger crushingly. 'Now we're going out hunting and you stay and cook the dinner.'

'All right,' said Violet Elizabeth obligingly. 'Kith me goodbye.'

Ginger stared at her in horror.

'But you mutht,' she said, 'if you're going out to work an' I'm going to cook the dinner, you mutht kith me goodbye. They do.'

'I don't,' said Ginger.

She held up her small face.

'*Pleath*, Ginger.'

Blushing to his ears Ginger just brushed her cheek with his. William gave a derisive snort. His self-respect had returned. Douglas's manly severity had been overborne. Ginger had been prevailed upon to kiss her. Well, they couldn't laugh at him now. They jolly *well* couldn't. Both were avoiding his eye.

'Well, go off to work, dear William and Douglas and Ginger,' said Violet Elizabeth happily, 'an' I'll cook.'

Gladly the hunters set off.

*

The Red Indian game had palled. It had been a success while it lasted. Ginger had brought some matches and over her purple layer of blackberry juice the faithful squaw now wore a layer of black from the very smoky fire they had at last managed to make.

'Come on,' said William, 'let's set out looking for adventures.'

They set off single file as before, Violet Elizabeth bringing up the rear, Jumble darting about in ecstatic searches for imaginary rabbits. Another small bog glimmered ahead. Violet Elizabeth, drunk with her success as a squaw, gave a scream.

'Another thquithy plath,' she cried. 'I want to be firtht.'

She flitted ahead of them, ran to the bog, slipped and fell into it face forward.

She arose at once. She was covered in black mud from head to foot. Her face was a black mud mask. Through it her teeth flashed in a smile. 'I juth thlipped,' she explained.

A man's voice came suddenly from the main path through the wood at their right.

'Look at 'em – the young rascals! Look at 'em! An' a dawg! Blarst 'em! Er-r-r-r-r!'

The last was a sound expressive of rage and threatening.

'Keepers!' said William. 'Run for your lives, braves. Come on, Jumble.'

They fled through the thicket.

'Pleath,' gasped Violet Elizabeth in the rear, 'I can't run as fatht ath that.'

It was Ginger and Douglas who came back to hold her hands. For all that they ran fleetly, dashing through the undergrowth where the keepers found it difficult to follow, and dodging round trees. At last, breathlessly, they reached a clearing and in the middle of it a cottage as small and attractive as a fairy tale cottage. The door was open. It had an empty look. They could hear the keepers coming through the undergrowth shouting.

'Come in here,' gasped William. 'It's empty. Come in and hide till they've gone.'

The four ran into a spotlessly clean little kitchen, and Ginger closed the door. The cottage was certainly empty. There was not a sound.

'Ithn't it a thweet little houth?' panted Violet Elizabeth.

'Come upstairs,' said Douglas. 'They might look in here.'

The four, Jumble scrambling after them, clattered up the steep narrow wooden stairs and into a small and very clean bedroom.

'Look out of the window and see when they go

past,' commanded William, 'then we'll slip out and go back.'

Douglas peeped cautiously out of the window. He gave a gasp.

'They – they're not goin' past,' he said. 'They – they're comin' in at the door.'

The men's voices could be heard below.

'Comin' in here – the young rascals! Look at their foot-marks, see? What'll my old woman say when she gets home?'

'They've gone upstairs, too. Look at the marks. Blarst 'em!'

William went to the window, holding Jumble beneath his arm.

'We can easily climb down by this pipe,' he said quickly. 'Then we'll run back.'

He swung a leg over the window sill, prepared to descend with Jumble clinging round his neck, as Jumble was trained to do. Jumble's life consisted chiefly of an endless succession of shocks to the nerves.

Ginger and Douglas prepared to follow.

The men's footsteps were heard coming upstairs when a small voice said plaintively, 'Pleath – pleath, I can't do that. Pleath, you're not going to leave me, are you?'

William put back his foot.

'We – we can't leave her,' he said. Ginger and Douglas did not question their leader's decision. They stood in a row facing the door while the footsteps drew nearer.

The door burst open and the two keepers appeared.

'Now, yer young rascals – we've got yer!'

Into Mr Bott's library were ushered two keepers, each leading two children by the neck. One held two rough-looking boys. The other held a rough-looking boy and a rough-looking little girl. A dejected-looking mongrel followed the procession.

'Trespassin', sir,' said the first keeper, 'trespassin' an' adamagin' of the woods. Old 'ands, too. Seen 'em at it before but never caught 'em till now. An' a *dawg* too. It's an example making of they want, sir. They want prosecutin' if I may make so bold. A-damagin' of the woods and a-bringing of a dawg—'

Mr Bott who was new to squiredom and had little knowledge of what was expected of him and moreover was afflicted at the moment with severe private domestic worries, cast a harassed glance at the four children. His glance rested upon Violet Elizabeth without the faintest flicker of recognition. He did not recognise her. He knew Violet Elizabeth. He saw her at least once or almost once a day. He knew her quite well. He knew her by her ordered flaxen curls, pink and white face and immaculate bunchy skirts. He did not know this little creature with the torn, stained, bedraggled dress (there was nothing bunchy about it now) whose extremely dirty face could just be seen beneath the tangle of untidy hair that fell over her eyes. She watched him silently and cautiously. Just as he was going to speak Violet Elizabeth's nurse entered. It says much for Violet Elizabeth's disguise that her nurse only threw her a passing glance. Violet Elizabeth's nurse's eyes were red-rimmed.

'Please, sir, Mrs Bott says is there any news?'

'No,' said Mr Bott desperately. 'Tell her I've rung up the police every minute since she sent last. How is she?'

'Please, sir, she's in hysterics again.'

Mr Bott groaned.

Ever since Violet Elizabeth's disappearance Mrs Bott had been indulging in hysterics in her bedroom and taking it out on Violet Elizabeth's nurse. In return Violet Elizabeth's nurse had hysterics in the nursery and took it out on the nursery maid. In return the nursery maid had hysterics in the kitchen and took it out on the kitchen maid. The kitchen maid had no time for hysterics but she took it out on the cat.

'Please, sir, she says she's too ill to speak now. She told me to tell you so, sir.'

Mr Bott groaned again. Suddenly he turned to the four children and their keepers.

'You've got their names and addresses, haven't you? Well, see here, children. Go out and see if you can find my little gal for me. She's lost. Look in the woods and round the village and – everywhere. And if you find her I'll let you off. See?'

They murmured perfunctory thanks and retired, followed by Violet Elizabeth who had not uttered one word within her paternal mansion.

In the woods they turned on her sternly.

'It's you he wants. You're her.'

'Yeth,' agreed the tousled ragamuffin who was Violet Elizabeth, sweetly, 'ith me.'

'Well, we're going to find you an' take you back.'

'Oh, *pleath*, I don't want to be found and tooken back. I like being with you.'

'Well, we can't keep you about with us all day, can we?' argued William sternly. 'You've gotter go home sometime same as we've gotter go home sometime. Well, we jolly well want our dinner now and we're jolly well going home an' we're jolly well goin' to take you home. He might give us something and—'

'All right,' agreed Violet Elizabeth holding up her face, 'if you'll all kith me I'll be found an' tooken back.'

*

The four of them stood again before Mr Bott's desk.

William and Ginger and Douglas took a step back and Violet Elizabeth took a step forward.

'We've found her,' said William.

'Where?' said Mr Bott looking round.

'Ith me,' piped Violet Elizabeth.

Mr Bott started.

'You?' he repeated in amazement.

'Yeth, Father, ith me.'

'But, but – God bless my soul—' he ejaculated peering at the unfamiliar apparition. 'It's impossible.'

Then he rang for Violet Elizabeth's nurse.

'Is this Violet Elizabeth?' he said.

'Yeth, ith me,' said Violet Elizabeth again.

Violet Elizabeth's nurse pushed back the tangle of hair.

'Oh, the poor poor child!' she cried. 'The poor child!'

'God bless my soul,' said Mr Bott again. 'Take her away. I don't know what you do to her, but do it and don't let her mother see her till it's done, and you boys stay here.'

'Oh, my lamb!' sobbed Violet Elizabeth's nurse as she led her away. 'My poor lamb!'

In an incredibly short time they returned. The mysterious something had been done. Violet Elizabeth's head was a mass of curls. Her face shone with cleanliness. Dainty lace-trimmed skirts stuck out ballet-dancer-wise beneath the pale blue waistband. Mr Bott took a deep breath.

'Now fetch her mother,' he said.

Like a tornado entered Mrs Bott. She still heaved with hysterics. She enfolded Violet Elizabeth to her visibly palpitating bosom.

'My child,' she sobbed. 'Oh my darling child.'

'I wath a thquaw,' said Violet Elizabeth. 'It dothn't make any thort of a noith. Ith a lady.'

'How did you—?' began Mrs Bott still straining Violet Elizabeth to her.

'These boys found her—' said Mr Bott.

'Oh, how kind – how noble,' said Mrs Bott. 'And one's that nice little boy who played with her so sweetly yesterday. Give them ten shillings each, Botty.'

'Well, but—' hesitated Mr Bott remembering the circumstances in which they had been brought to him.

'Botty!' screamed Mrs Bott tearfully, 'don't you value your darling child's life at even thirty shillings?'

Hastily Mr Bott handed them each a ten-shilling note.

They tramped homewards by the road.

'Well, it's turned out all right,' said Ginger lugubriously, but fingering the ten-shilling note in his pocket, 'but it

'WE'VE FOUND HER,' ANNOUNCED WILLIAM, AND VIOLET
ELIZABETH TOOK A STEP FORWARD. 'ITH ME,' SHE PIPED.

might not have. 'Cept for the money it jolly well spoilt the
morning.'

'Girls always do,' said William. 'I'm not going to have
anything to do with any ole girl ever again.'

'GOD BLESS MY SOUL!' EXCLAIMED MR BOTT, PEERING AT
THE APPARITION. 'IT'S IMPOSSIBLE.'

''S all very well sayin' that,' said Douglas who had
been deeply impressed that morning by the inevitableness
and deadly persistence of the sex, ''s all very well sayin'
that. It's them what has to do with you.'

'An' I'm never goin' to marry any ole girl,' said William.

''S all very well sayin' *that*,' said Douglas again gloomily, 'but some ole girl'll probably marry you.'

CHAPTER 4

WILLIAM TURNS OVER A NEW LEAF

William had often been told how much happier he would be if he would follow the straight and narrow path of virtue, but so far the thought of that happiness had left him cold. He preferred the happiness that he knew by experience to be the result of his normal wicked life to that mythical happiness that was prophesied as the result of a quite unalluring life of righteousness. Suddenly, however, he was stirred. An 'old boy' had come to visit the school and had given an inspiring address to the boys in which he spoke of the beauty and usefulness of a life of Self-denial and Service. William, for the first time, began to consider the question seriously. He realised that his life so far had not been, strictly speaking, a life of Self-denial and Service. The 'old boy' said many things that impressed William. He pictured the liver of the life of Self-denial and Service surrounded by a happy, grateful and admiring family circle. He said that everyone would love such a character. William tried to imagine his own family circle as a happy, grateful and admiring family circle. It was not an easy task even to such a vivid imagination as William's but it was not altogether impossible. After all, nothing was altogether impossible . . .

While the headmaster was proposing a vote of thanks to the eloquent and perspiring 'old boy', William was deciding that there might be something in the idea after all. When the bell rang for the end of school, William had decided that it was worth trying at any rate. He decided to start first thing next morning – not before. William was a good organiser. He liked things cut and dried. A new day for a new life. It was no use beginning to be self-denying and self-sacrificing in the middle of a day that had started quite differently. If you were going to have a beautiful character and a grateful family circle you might as well start the day fresh with it, not drag it over from the day before. It would be jolly nice to have a happy, grateful and admiring family circle, and William only hoped that if he took the trouble to be self-denying and self-sacrificing his family circle would take the trouble to be happy and grateful and admiring. There were dark doubts about this in William's mind. His family circle rarely did anything that was expected of them. Still, William was an optimist and – anything might happen. And tomorrow was a whole holiday. He could give all his attention to it all day . . .

He looked forward to the new experience with feelings of pleasant anticipation. It would be interesting and jolly – meantime there was a whole half of today left and it was no use beginning the life of self-denial and service before the scheduled time.

He joined his friends Ginger, Henry and Douglas after school and together they trespassed on the lands of the most irascible farmer they knew in the hopes of a pleasant chase. The farmer happened to be in the market town so their hopes were disappointed as far as he was concerned. They paddled in his pond and climbed his trees and uttered defiant shouts to his infuriated dog, and were finally chased away by his wife with a fire of hard and knobbly potatoes. One got William very nicely on the side of his head but, his head being as hard and knobbly as the potato, little damage was done. Next they 'scouted' each other through the village and finally went into Ginger's house and performed military manoeuvres in Ginger's bedroom, till Ginger's mother sent them away because the room just below happened to be the drawing-room and the force of the military manoeuvres was disintegrating the ceiling and sending it down in picturesque white flakes into Ginger's mother's hair.

They went next to Henry's garden and there with much labour made a bonfire. Ginger and Douglas plied the fire

69

with fuel; and William and Henry, with a wheelbarrow and the garden hose, wearing old tins on their heads, impersonated the fire brigade. During the exciting scuffles that followed, the garden hose became slightly involved and finally four dripping boys fled from the scene and from possible detection, leaving only the now swimming bonfire, the wheelbarrow and hose to mark the scene of action. A long rest in a neighbouring field in the still blazing sunshine soon partially dried them. While reclining at ease they discussed the latest Red Indian stories which they had read, and the possibility of there being any wild animals left in England.

'I bet there *is*,' said Ginger earnestly. 'They hide in the day time so's no one'll see 'em, an' they come out at nights. No one goes into the woods at night so no one knows if there is or if there isn't, an' I bet there *is*. Anyway, let's get up some night 'n take our bows 'n arrows an' *look* for 'em. I bet we'd find some.'

'Let's tonight,' said Douglas eagerly.

William remembered suddenly the life of virtue to which he had mentally devoted himself. He felt that the nocturnal hunting for wild animals was incompatible with it.

'I can't tonight,' he said with an air of virtue.

'Yah – you're *'fraid*!' taunted Henry, not because he

had the least doubt of William's courage but simply to introduce an element of excitement into the proceedings.

He succeeded.

When finally Henry and William arose breathless and bruised from the ditch where the fight had ended, Douglas and Ginger surveyed them with dispassionate interest.

'William won an' you're both in a *jolly* old mess!'

Henry removed some leaves and bits of grass from his mouth.

'All right, you're *not* afraid,' he said pacifically to William, 'when will you come huntin' wild animals?'

William considered. He was going to give the life of virtue, of self-denial and service a fair day's trial, but there was just the possibility that from William's point of view it might not be a success. It would be as well to leave the door to the old life open.

'I'll tell you tomorrow,' he said guardedly.

'All right. I say, let's race to the end of the field on only one leg . . . Come on! Ready . . . One, two, *three* . . . GO!'

II

William awoke. It was morning. It was the morning on which he was to begin his life of self-denial and service. He raised his voice in one of his penetrating and tuneless morning songs, then stopped abruptly, 'case I disturb anyone' he remarked virtuously to his brush and comb . . . His father frequently remarked that William's early morning songs were enough to drive a man to drink . . . He brushed his hair with unusual vigour and descended to breakfast looking (for William) unusually sleek and virtuous. His father was reading the paper in front of the fire.

'Good mornin', Father,' said William in a voice of suave politeness.

His father grunted.

'Did you hear me not singin' this mornin', Father?' said William pleasantly. It was as well that his self-denials should not be missed by the family circle.

His father did not answer. William sighed. Some family circles were different from others. It was hard to imagine his father happy and grateful and admiring. But still, he was going to have a jolly good try . . .

His mother and sister and brother came down. William said 'Good mornin'!' to them all with unctuous affability. His brother looked at him suspiciously.

'What mischief are *you* up to?' he said ungraciously.

William merely gave him a long, silent and reproachful glance.

'What are you going to do this morning, William dear?' said his mother.

72

'I don' mind what I do,' said William. 'I jus' want to *help* you. I'll do anything you like, Mother.'

She looked at him anxiously.

'Are you feeling quite well, dear?' she said with concern.

'If you want to *help*,' said his sister sternly, 'you might dig up that piece of my garden you and those other boys trampled down yesterday.'

William decided that a life of self-denial and service need not include fagging for sisters who spoke to one in that tone of voice. He pretended not to hear.

'Can I do anything at all for you this morning, Mother dear?' he said earnestly.

His mother looked too taken aback to reply. His father rose and folded up his newspaper.

'Take my advice,' he said, 'and beware of that boy this morning. He's up to something!'

William sighed again. Some family circles simply didn't seem able to recognise a life of self-denial and service when they met it . . .

After breakfast he wandered into the garden. Before long Ginger, Douglas and Henry came down the road.

'Come on, William!' they called over the gate.

For a moment William was tempted. Somehow it seemed a terrible waste of a holiday to spend it in self-denial and service instead of in search of adventures with

Ginger, Douglas and Henry. But he put the temptation away. When he made up his mind to do a thing he did it . . .

'Can't come today,' he said sternly, 'I'm busy.'

'Oh, *go on*!'

'Well, I am an' I'm just not comin' an' kin'ly stop throwin' stones at our cat.'

'Call it a cat! Thought it was an ole fur glove what someone'd thrown away!'

In furious defence of his household's cat (whose life William in private made a misery) William leapt to the gate. The trio fled down the road. William returned to his meditations. His father had gone to business and Ethel and Robert had gone to golf. His mother drew up the morning-room window.

'William, darling, aren't you going to play with your friends this morning?'

William turned to her with an expression of solemnity and earnestness.

'I want to *help* you, Mother. I don't wanter play with my friends.'

He felt a great satisfaction with this speech. It breathed the very spirit of self-denial and service.

'I'll try to find that bottle of tonic you didn't finish after whooping cough,' said his mother helplessly as she drew down the window.

William stared around him disconsolately. It was hard to be full of self-sacrifices and service and to find no outlet for it . . . nobody seemed to want his help. Then a brilliant idea occurred to him. He would *do* something for each of his family – something that would be a pleasant surprise when they found out . . .

He went up to his bedroom. There in a drawer was a poem that he had found in Robert's blotter the week before. It began:

> O Marion
> So young and fair
> With silken hair . . .

It must be Marion Dexter. She was fair and, well, more or less young, William supposed. William didn't know about her hair being silken. It looked just like ordinary hair to him. But you never knew with girls. He had kept the poem in order to use it as a weapon of offence against Robert when occasion demanded. But that episode belonged to his old evil past. In his new life of self-denial and service he wanted to *help* Robert. The poem ended:

> I should be happy, I aver
> If thou my suit wouldst but prefer.

That meant that Robert wanted to be engaged to her. Poor Robert! Perhaps he was too shy to ask her, or perhaps he'd asked her and she'd refused . . . well, it was here that Robert needed some *help*. William, with a determined expression, set off down the road.

III

He knocked loudly at the door. By a lucky chance Marion Dexter came to the door herself.

'Good afternoon,' she said.

'Good afternoon,' said William in a business-like fashion. 'Has Robert ever asked you to marry him?'

'No. What a peculiar question to ask on the front doorstep. Do come in.'

William followed her into the drawing-room. She shut the door. They both sat down. William's face was set and frowning.

'He's deep in love with you,' he said in a conspiratorial whisper.

Marion's eyes danced.

'Did he send you to tell me?'

William ignored the question.

'He's deep in love with you and wants you to marry him.'

Marion dimpled.

'Why can't he ask me then?'

'He's shy,' said William earnestly, 'he's always shy when he's in love. He's always awful shy with the people what he's in love with. But he wants most *awful* bad to marry you. *Do* marry him, *please*. Jus' for kindness. I'm tryin' to be kind. That's why I'm here.'

'I see,' she said. 'Are you sure he's in love with me?'

'Deep in love. Writin' po'try an' carryin' on – not sleepin' and not eatin' an' murmurin' your name an' puttin' his hand on his heart an' carvin' your initials all over the house an' sendin' you flowers an' things,' said William drawing freely on his imagination.

'I've never had any flowers from him.'

'No. They all get lost in the post,' said William without turning a hair. 'But he's dyin' slow of love for you. He's gettin' thinner an' thinner. 'F you don't be engaged to him soon he'll be stone dead. He'll die of love like what they do in tales an' then you'll probably get hung for murder.'

'Good heavens!' said Miss Dexter.

'Well, I *hope* you won't,' said William kindly, 'an' I'll do all I can to save you if you are but 'f you kill Robert with not gettin' engaged to him prob'ly you will be.'

'Does he know you've come to ask me?' said Miss Dexter.

'GOOD HEAVENS!' SAID MISS DEXTER. 'DOES HE KNOW
YOU'VE COME TO ASK ME?'

'ROBERT'S DEEP IN LOVE WITH YOU,' SAID WILLIAM. 'HE'S
WRITIN' PO'TRY AN' NOT SLEEPIN' AN' NOT EATIN' AND
CARVIN' YOUR INITIALS ALL OVER THE HOUSE.'

'No. I want it to be a s'prise to him,' said William.

'It will be that,' murmured Miss Dexter.

'You will marry him, then?' said William hopefully.

'Certainly – if he wants me to.'

'P'raps,' said William after a slight pause, 'you'd better write it in a letter 'cause he'd like as not, not b'lieve me.'

With eyes dancing and lips quivering with suppressed laughter Miss Dexter sat down at her writing-table.

DEAR ROBERT (she wrote),

At William's earnest request I promise to be engaged to you and to marry you whenever you like.

Yours sincerely, MARION DEXTER.

She handed it to William. William read it gravely and put it in his pocket.

'Thanks ever so much,' he said fervently.

'Don't mention it,' said Miss Dexter demurely. 'Quite a pleasure.'

He walked down the road in a rosy glow of virtue. Well, he'd done something for Robert that ought to make Robert grateful to him for the rest of his life. He'd *helped* Robert all right. He'd like to know what *service* was if it wasn't that – getting people engaged to people they wanted to be engaged to. Jolly hard work too. Now there remained his mother and Ethel. He must go home and try to find some way of *helping* them . . .

IV

When he reached home Ethel was showing out Mrs Helm, a tall, stern-looking lady whom William knew by sight.

'I'm so *frightfully* disappointed not to be able to come,' Ethel was saying regretfully, 'but I'm afraid I *must* go to the Morrisons. I promised over a week ago. Thank you so much for asking me. Good morning.'

William followed her into the dining-room where his mother was.

'What did she want, dear?' said Mrs Brown. 'Go and wash your hands, William.'

'She wanted me to go in this evening but I told her I couldn't because I was going to the Morrisons. Thank Heaven I had an excuse!'

William unfortunately missed the last sentence as, still inspired by high ideals of virtue, he had gone at once upstairs to wash his hands. While he splashed about at the handbasin an idea suddenly occurred to him. *That* was how he'd help Ethel. He'd give her a happy evening. She should spend it with the Helms and not with the Morrisons. She'd sounded so sorry that she had to go to the Morrisons and couldn't go to the Helms. He'd fix it all up for her this afternoon. He'd *help* her like he'd helped Robert.

He had hoped to be able to give Robert Miss Dexter's note at lunch, but it turned out that Robert was lunching at the golf club with a friend.

Directly after lunch William set off to Mrs Morrison's house. He was shown into the drawing-room. Mrs Morrison, large and fat and comfortable-looking, entered. She looked rather bewildered as she met William's stern frowning gaze.

'I've come from Ethel,' said William aggressively. 'She's sorry she can't come tonight.'

Mrs Morrison's cheerful countenance fell.

'The girls will be disappointed,' she said, 'they saw her this morning and she said she was looking forward to it.'

Some explanation seemed necessary. William was never one to stick at half measures.

'She's been took ill since then,' he said.

'Oh *dear*,' said Mrs Morrison with concern, 'nothing serious, I hope?'

William considered. If it wasn't serious she might expect Ethel to recover by the evening. She'd better have something serious.

'I'm 'fraid it is,' he said gloomily.

'Dear, *dear*!' said Mrs Morrison. 'Tch! Tch! What is it?'

William thought over all the complaints he knew. None of them seemed quite serious enough. She might as well have something *really* serious while he was about it. Then he suddenly remembered hearing the gardener talking to the housemaid the day before. He'd been talking about his brother who'd got – what was it? Epi – epi—

'Epilepsy!' said William suddenly.

'*What?*' screamed Mrs Morrison.

William, having committed himself to epilepsy meant to stick to it.

'Epilepsy, the doctor says,' he said firmly.

'Good heavens!' said Mrs Morrison. 'When did you find out? Will he be able to cure it? Is the poor girl in bed? How does it affect her? What a dreadful thing!'

William was flattered at the impression he seemed to have made. He wondered whether it were possible to increase it.

'The doctor thinks she's got a bit of consumption too,' he said casually, 'but he's not quite sure.'

Mrs Morrison screamed again. '*Heavens!* And she always looked so *healthy*. The girls will be so *distressed*. William, do tell me – when did your mother realise there was something wrong?'

William foresaw that the conversation was becoming complicated. He did not wish to display his ignorance of the symptoms of epilepsy and consumption.

'Jus' soon after lunch,' he said with rising cheerfulness. 'Now I'd better be goin', I think. Good afternoon.'

He left Mrs Morrison still gasping upon the sofa and in the act of ringing for her maid to fetch her smelling salts.

William walked down the road with a swagger. He was managing *jolly* well . . . The next visit was easier. He simply told Mrs Helm's maid at the front door to tell Mrs Helm that Ethel would be able to come tonight after all, thank you very much.

Then he swung off to the woods with Jumble, his faithful dog. In accordance with his new life of virtue he walked straight along the road without burrowing in the ditches or throwing stones at telegraph posts. His exhilaration slowly vanished. He wondered where Ginger and Henry and Douglas were and what they were doing. It was *jolly* dull all alone . . . but still the happiness and gratitude and admiration of his family circle when they found out all he had done for them would repay him for everything. At least he hoped it would. His mother . . . he had done nothing for his mother yet. He must try to do something for his mother . . .

v

When he returned home it was almost dinner time. His mother and Ethel and Robert were still out. The Cook met him with a lugubrious face.

'Now, Master William,' she said, 'can I trust you to give a message to your ma?'

'Yes, Cook,' said William virtuously.

'Me cold in me 'ead's that bad I can't stand on me feet no longer. That 'ussy Ellen wouldn't give up 'er night hout to 'elp me – not she, and yer ma said if I'd leave things orl ready to dish hup I might go and rest afore dinner 'f I felt bad. Well, she'll be hin hany minute now and just tell 'er it's hall ready to dish up. Tell 'er I 'aven't made no pudd'n but I've hopened a bottle of stewed pears.'

'All right, Cook,' said William.

Cook took the paperback copy of *A Mill Girl's Romance* from the kitchen dresser and slowly sneezed her way up the back stairs.

William was to all intents and purposes alone in the house. He wandered into the kitchen. There was a pleasant smell of cooking. Several saucepans simmered on the gas stove. On the table was a glass dish containing the stewed pears. His father hated cold stewed fruit. He often said so. Suddenly William had yet another brilliant idea. He'd make a proper pudding for his father. It wouldn't

85

take long. The cookery book was on the dresser. You just did what the book told you. It was quite easy.

He went over to the gas stove. All the gas rings were being used. He'd better get one clear for his pudding. He supposed his pudding would need a gas ring same as all the other things. There were two small saucepans each containing dark brown stuff. They might as well be together, thought William, with a business-like frown. He poured the contents of one of the saucepans into the other. He had a moment's misgiving as the mingled smell of gravy and coffee arose from the mixture. Then he turned to his pudding. He opened the book at random at the puddings. Any would do. 'Beat three eggs together.' He fetched a bowl of eggs from the larder and got down a clean basin from the shelf. He'd seen Cook doing it, just cracking the eggs, and the egg slithered into the basin and she threw the shells away. It looked quite easy. He broke an egg. The shell fell neatly on to the table and the egg slithered down William on to the floor. He tried another and the same thing happened. William was not easily baulked. He was of a persevering nature. He went on breaking eggs till not another egg remained to be broken, and then and then only did he relinquish his hopes of making a pudding. Then and then only did he step out of the pool of a dozen broken eggs in which he was standing

WILLIAM WENT ON BREAKING EGGS TILL NOT ANOTHER
EGG REMAINED TO BE BROKEN.

and, literally soaked in egg from the waist downward, go to replace the basin on the shelf.

His thirst for practical virtue was not yet sated. Surely there was *something* he could do, even if he couldn't make a pudding. Yes, he could carry the things into the dining-room so that they could have dinner as soon as they came in. He opened the oven door. A chicken on a large dish was there. Good! Burning his fingers severely in the process William took it out. He'd put it on the dining-room table all ready for them to begin. Just as he stood with the dish in his hands he heard his mother and Robert come in. He'd go and give Robert Miss Dexter's letter first. He looked round for somewhere to put the chicken. The table seemed to be full. He put the dish and the chicken on to the floor and went into the hall closing the door behind him. Robert and his mother had gone into the drawing-room. William followed.

'Well, William,' said Mrs Brown pleasantly, 'had a nice day?'

Without a word William handed the note to Robert.

Robert read it.

He went first red, then pale, then a wild look came into his eyes.

'Marion *Dexter*!' he said.

'You're in love with her, aren't you?' said William. 'You've been writing pomes to her.'

'Not to Marion *Dexter*,' screamed Robert. 'She's an old woman. She's nearly twenty-five . . . It's – Marion Hatherley I—'

'Well, how was I to *know*?' said William in a voice of irritation. 'You should put their surnames in the pomes. I thought you wanted to be engaged to her. I've took a lot of trouble over it gettin' her to write that.'

Robert was reading and re-reading the note.

'My God!' he said in a hushed voice of horror. 'I'm engaged to Marion Dexter!'

'Robert,' said Mrs Brown. 'I don't think you ought to use expressions like that before your little brother, whoever you're engaged to.'

'I'm engaged to Marion Dexter,' repeated Robert in a tone of frenzy, '*Me!* . . . chained to her for life when I love another . . .'

'Robert dear,' said Mrs Brown, 'if there's been any mistake I'm sure that all you have to do is to go to Miss Dexter and explain.'

'*Explain!*' said Robert wildly. 'How can I explain? She's *accepted* me . . . How can any man of chivalry refuse to marry a woman who? . . . Oh, it's too much.' He sat down on the sofa and held his head in his hands. 'It's the ruin of all my hopes . . . he's simply spoilt my life . . . he's always spoiling my life . . . I shall *have* to marry her now . . . and she's an old woman . . . she was twenty-four last birthday, I know.'

'Well, I was trying to *help*,' said William.

'I'll teach you to help,' said Robert darkly, advancing upon him.

William dodged and fled towards the door. There he collided with Ethel – Ethel with a pale, distraught face.

'It's all over the village, Mother,' she said angrily as she entered. 'William's told everyone in the village that I've got epilepsy and consumption.'

'I *didn't*,' said William indignantly. 'I only told Mrs Morrison.'

'But, William,' said his mother, sitting down weakly on the nearest chair, 'why on earth—?'

'Well, Ethel didn't want to go to the Morrisons tonight. She wanted to go to the Helms—'

'I did *not*,' said Ethel. 'I was glad to get out of going to the Helms.'

'Well, how was I to *know*?' said William desperately. 'I had to go by what you *said* and I had to go by what Robert *wrote*. I wanted to *help*. I've took no end of trouble – livin' a life of self-sacrifice and service all day without stoppin' once, and 'stead of being grateful an' happy an' admirin'—'

90

'But, William,' said Mrs Brown, 'how did you think it was going to help *anyone* to say that Ethel had epilepsy and consumption?'

'I'd rather have epilepsy and consumption,' said Robert who had returned to the sofa and was sitting with his head between his hands, 'than be engaged to Marion Dexter.'

'I must say I simply can't understand why you've been doing all this, William,' said Mrs Brown. 'We must just wait till your father comes in and see what he makes of it. And I can't think why dinner's so late.'

'She's gone to bed,' said William gloomily.

'I'd better see to things then,' said Mrs Brown going into the hall.

'*Epilepsy!*' groaned Ethel.

'Twenty-four – twenty-four if she's a day – and the sort of hair I've always disliked,' groaned Robert.

William followed his mother to the kitchen rather than be left to the tender mercies of Ethel and Robert. He began to feel distinctly apprehensive about the kitchen . . . that pool of eggs . . . those brown liquids he'd mixed . . .

Mrs Brown opened the kitchen door. On the empty chicken dish on the floor sat Jumble surrounded by chicken bones, the wishing bone protruding from his mouth, looking blissfully happy . . .

VI

In his bedroom whither he had perforce retired supperless, William hung up the Outlaw's signal of distress (a scull and crossbones in black and the word 'Help' in red) at his window in case Ginger or Henry or Douglas came down the road, and then surveyed the events of the day. Well, he'd done his best. He'd lived a life of self-denial and service all right. It was his family who were wrong. They hadn't been happy or grateful or admiring. They simply weren't worthy of a life of self-denial and service. And anyway how could he have *known* that it was another Marion and that Ethel couldn't say what she meant and that Jumble was going to get in through the kitchen window?

A tiny pebble hit his window. He threw it open. There down below in the garden path were Douglas, Henry and Ginger.

'Ho! My trusty mates,' said William in a penetrating whisper. 'I am pent in durance vile – sent to bed, you know – an' I'm jolly hungry. Wilt kill some deer or venison or something for me?'

'Righto,' said Ginger, and 'Yes, gallant captain,' said Douglas and Henry as they crept off through the bushes.

William returned to his survey of his present position. That old boy simply didn't know what he was talking about. He couldn't ever have tried it himself. Anyway he (William) had tried it and he knew all there was to know about lives of self-denial and service and he'd *done* with lives of self-denial and service, thank you very much. He was going back to his ordinary kind of life first thing tomorrow . . .

A tiny pebble at the window. William leant out. Below were Ginger, Henry and Douglas with a small basket.

'Oh, crumbs!' said William joyfully.

He lowered a string and they tied the little basket on to it. William drew it up fairly successfully. It contained a half-eaten apple, a bar of toffee that had spent several days unwrapped in Henry's pocket, which was covered with bits of fluff, a very stale bun purloined from Ginger's mother's larder, and a packet of monkey nuts bought with Ginger's last twopence.

William's eyes shone.

'Oh, I *say*,' he said gratefully, 'thanks *awfully*. And, I say, you'd better go now 'case they see you, and I *say*, I'll come huntin' wild animals with you tomorrow night.'

'Righto,' said the Outlaws creeping away through the bushes.

Downstairs William's family circle consumed a meal consisting of sardines and stewed pears. They consumed it in gloomy silence, broken only by Mr Brown's dry, 'I suppose there must be quite a heavy vein of insanity somewhere in the family for it to come out so strongly in William.' And by Ethel's indignant, 'And *epilepsy*! Why on earth did he fix on *epilepsy*?' And by Robert's gloomy, 'Engaged to be married to her . . . *twenty-four* . . . *chained* to her for life.'

Upstairs the cause of all their troubles sat on the floor in the middle of his bedroom with his little pile of eatables before him.

'Come on, my gallant braves,' he said addressing an imaginary band of fellow captives. 'Let us eat well and then devise some way of escape or ere dawn our bleached bones may dangle from yon gallows.'

Then quite happily and contentedly he began to eat the fluffy stick of toffee . . .

CHAPTER 5

A BIT OF BLACKMAIL

Bob Andrews was one of the picturesque figures of the village. He lived at the East Lodge of the Hall, and was supposed to help with the gardening of the Hall grounds. He was tall, handsome, white-bearded and gloriously lazy. He had a roguish twinkle in his blue eyes and a genius for wasting time – both his own and other people's. He was a great friend of William and the Outlaws. He seemed to them to be free of all the drawbacks that usually accompany the state of grown-upness. He was never busy, never disapproving, never tidy, never abstracted. He took seriously the really important things of life such as cigarette-card collecting, the top season, Red Indians, and the finding of birds' nests. Having abstracted a promise from them that they would take 'one igg an' no more, ye rascals', he would show them every bird's nest in the Hall woods. He seemed to know exactly where each bird would build each year. He had a family of two tame squirrels, four dogs and seven cats, who all lived together in unity. He could carve boats out of wood, make whistles and bows and arrows and tops. He did all these things as if he had nothing else to do in the world. He would stand for hours perfectly happy with his hands in his pockets, smoking. He would watch the Outlaws organising races of boats, watch them shooting their bows and arrows, taking interest in their marksmanship, offering helpful criticism. He was in every way an eminently satisfactory person. He was paid a regular salary by the absent owner of the Hall for occasionally opening the Lodge gates, and still more occasionally assisting with the gardening. He understood the word assistance in its most literal sense – that of 'standing by'. He was also generous with kindly advice to his more active colleagues. It says much for his attractive personality that this want of activity was resented by no one.

Mr Bott, the new owner of the Hall, was a businessman. He liked to get his money's worth for his money. It was not for nothing that passionate appeals to safeguard their health by taking Bott's Sauce with every meal met England's citizens in every town. Mr Bott believed in getting the last ounce of work out of his work-people. That was what had raised Mr Bott from grocer's errand boy to lord of the manor. When Mr Bott discovered that he had upon his newly acquired estate a man who drew a working man's salary for merely standing about and at intervals consuming the more choice fruit from the hothouses, Mr Bott promptly sacked that man. It would have been against Mr Bott's most sacred principles to do otherwise . . .

The Outlaws avoided Mr Bott's estate for some time after their adventure with his daughter. But having heard that she had departed on a lengthy visit to distant relatives, the Outlaws decided to return to their favourite haunts. They entered the wood by crawling through the hedge. For a time they amused themselves by climbing trees and turning somersaults among the leaves. Then they tried jumping over the stream. The stream possessed the attraction of being just too wide to jump over. The interest lay in seeing how much or how little of their boots got wet each time. Finally the Outlaws wearied of these pursuits.

'Let's go and find Bob,' said William at last.

Scuffling, shuffling, dragging their toes along the ground, whistling, punching each other at intervals, in the fashion of boyhood, they made their way slowly to the East Lodge.

Bob stood at his door smoking as usual.

'Hello, Bob,' called the Outlaws.

'Hello, ye young rascals.'

'I say, Bob, make us some boats an' let's have a race.'

'Sure an' I will,' said Bob knocking out his pipe and taking a large penknife out of his pocket, 'though it's wastin' me time ye are, as usual.'

He took up a piece of wood and began to whittle.

'How's the squirrel, Bob?'

'Foine.'

'Bob, they're building in the ivy on the Old Oak again.'

'Shure an' I knew that before you did, me bhoy.'

But though he whittled and whistled Bob was evidently not his old self.

'I say, Bob, next month—'

'Next month, me bhoys, I shall not be here.'

They stared at him open-mouthed.

'*What* – you goin' away for a holiday, Bob?'

Bob whittled away nonchalantly.

'I'm goin' away, me bhoys, because th'ould devil up there has given me the sack – God forgive him for *Oi* won't,' he ended piously.

'But – *why*?' they said, aghast.

'He sez I don't work. *Me!*' he said indignantly. '*Me* – an' me wearin' me hands to the bone for him the way I do. *An'* he says I steal 'is fruit – me what takes only the few peaches he'd come an' give me with his own hands if he was a gintleman at all, at all.'

'What a *shame*!' said the Outlaws.

'Turnin' me an' me hanimals out into the cold world. May God forgive him!' said Bob. 'Well, here's yer boats, ye young rascals, an' don't ye go near me pheasants' nests or I'll put the fear of God on ye.'

'We've gotter *do* something,' said William, when Bob had returned, smoking peacefully, to his Lodge.

'*We* can't do anything,' said Ginger despondently. 'Who'd listen to *us*? Who'd take any notice of *us*, anyway?'

William the leader looked at him sternly.

'You jus' wait an' *see*,' he said.

Mr Bott was very stout. His stoutness was a great secret trouble to Mr Bott. Mr Bott had made his money and now Mr Bott wished to take his proper place in Society. Mr Bott considered not unreasonably that his corpulency, though an excellent advertisement of the nourishing qualities of Bott's Sauce, yet detracted from the refinement of his appearance. Mrs Bott frequently urged him to 'do something about it'. He had consulted many expensive specialists. Mrs Bott kept finding 'new men' for him. The last 'new man' she had found was highly recommended on all sides. He practically guaranteed his treatment to transform a human balloon to a human pencil in a few months. Mr Bott had begun the treatment. It was irksome

but Mr Bott was persevering. Had Mr Bott not been persevering he would never have attained that position of eminence in the commercial world that he now held. Every morning as soon as it was light, Mr Bott, decently covered by a large overcoat, went down to a small lake in the grounds among the bushes. There Mr Bott divested himself of his overcoat and appeared in small bathing drawers. From the pocket of his overcoat Mr Bott would then take a skipping rope and with this he would skip five times round the lake. Then he would put away his skipping rope and do his exercises. He would twist his short fat body into strange attitudes, flinging his short fat arms towards Heaven, standing upon one short fat leg with the other thrust out at various angles and invariably overbalancing. Finally, Mr Bott had to plunge into the lake (it was not deep), splash and kick and run round in it, and then emerge to dry himself on a towel concealed in the other pocket of his overcoat, shiveringly don the overcoat again and furtively return to the house. For Mr Bott was shy about his 'treatment'. He fondly imagined that no one except Mrs Bott, the 'new man' and himself knew about his early morning adventures.

One chilly morning Mr Bott had skipped and leapt and twisted himself and splashed himself and emerged shivering and red-nosed for his overcoat. Then Mr Bott received a shock that was nearly too much for his much exercised system. His overcoat was not there. He looked all round the tree where he knew he had left it, and it was not there. It was most certainly not there. With chattering teeth Mr Bott threw a glance of pathetic despair around him. Then above the sound of the chattering of his teeth he heard a voice.

'I've got your coat up here.'

Mr Bott threw a startled glance up into the tree whence the voice came. From among the leaves a stern, freckled, snub-nosed, wild-haired face glared down at him.

'I'll give you your coat,' said William, ''f you'll promise to let Bob stay.'

Mr Bott clasped his dripping head with a dripping hand.

'Bob?'

'Bob Andrews what you're sending away for nothing.'

Mr Bott tried to look dignified in spite of the chattering of his teeth and the water that poured from his hair down his face.

'I have my reasons, child,' he said, 'of which you know nothing. Will you kindly give me back my coat? I'm afraid you are a very naughty, ill-behaved little boy to do a thing like this and if you aren't careful I'll tell the police about it.'

'I'll give you your coat if you'll promise not to send Bob away,' said William again sternly.

'I shall most certainly speak to your father *and* the police,' said Mr Bott. 'You're a very impudent little boy! Give me my coat at once.'

'I'll give you your coat,' said William again, 'if you'll promise not to send Bob away.'

Mr Bott's dignity began to melt away.

'You young devil,' he roared. 'You—'

He looked wildly around and his eyes fell upon something upon which William's eye ought to have fallen before. William had for once overlooked something vital to his strategy. In the long grass behind the tree lay a ladder that had been left there long ago by some gardener and forgotten. With a yell of triumph Mr Bott rushed to it.

'Oh, crumbs!' said William among the leafage.

Mr Bott put the ladder against the tree trunk and began to swarm up it – large, dripping, chattering with rage and cold. William retreated along his branch; still clinging to the overcoat. Mr Bott pursued furiously.

'You young rogue – you young devil. I'll teach you – I'll—'

The branch down which William was retreating pursued by Mr Bott was directly over the lake. William alone it could easily have supported, but it drew the line at Mr Bott. With a creaking and crashing above which rose a yell of terror from Mr Bott, it fell into the water accompanied by its two occupants. The splash made by Mr Bott's falling body at first obscured the landscape. Before William could recover from the shock caused by Mr Bott's splash and yell and his own unexpected descent, Mr Bott was upon him. Mr Bott was maddened by rage and fury, and wet and cold. He ducked William and shook William and tore his wet overcoat from William. William butted Mr Bott in his largest and roundest part, then scrambled from the lake and fled dripping towards the gate. Mr Bott at first pursued him, then realising that the path was taking him within sight of the high road, turned back, drew his soaked overcoat over his shoulders and fled chatteringly and shiveringly towards his resplendent mansion.

*

Two hours later, William met the other Outlaws by appointment in the old barn where all their meetings were held.

'Well?' said the other Outlaws eagerly.

William, who was wearing his best suit, looked pale and chastened but none the less determined.

'It didn't quite come off,' admitted William. 'Something went wrong.'

Their faces fell, but they did not question him.

'Well, we've done all we can,' said Ginger resignedly, 'an' we jus' can't help it.'

'I've got another idea,' said William grimly. 'I've jolly well not *finished* yet.'

They looked at him with awe and respect.

'We'll have another meeting in three days,' said William with his stern frown, 'an' – an' – well, you jus' wait and see.'

The next day was bright and sunny. Mr Bott almost enjoyed his morning exercises. He thought occasionally with indignation of the events of the previous morning. That dreadful boy . . . anyway he'd *shown* him – he wasn't likely to come again after yesterday. And most certainly Bob Andrews should go . . . he'd like to see any fool boy dictating to *him*. But Mr Bott could not feel bad-tempered for long. It was such a bright sunny morning and he'd just discovered himself to be ⅞ of an inch thinner round the waist than this time last week . . .

He leapt and skipped and gambolled and splashed. Once he imagined he saw the horrible boy's face in the bushes, but looking again he came to the conclusion that he must have been mistaken. Once too, he thought he heard a snap or a click as if someone had stepped on a twig, but listening again he came to the conclusion that he must have been mistaken. He enjoyed his exercises for the next two mornings as well. But on the third morning as soon as he had come down, dressed and glowing, to his study after his exercises, to look at his letters before breakfast the butler threw open the door and announced:

'They said it was himportant business, sir, an' you knew about it. I 'ope it's all right.'

Then four boys walked up to his desk. One was the boy who had taken his overcoat up a tree two days before. The butler had gone. Mr Bott, sputtering with rage, reached out to the bell. He was going to say 'Kick these boys out', when the worst of the boys – the devil – laid half a dozen snapshots on his desk. Mr Bott looked at them, and then sat rigid and motionless, his hand still outstretched towards the bell.

Then his rubicund face grew pale.

The first snapshot showed Mr Bott, short, fat, and

ONCE MR BOTT THOUGHT HE SAW THAT HORRIBLE BOY'S
FACE IN THE BUSHES. ONCE HE IMAGINED HE HEARD AN
ODD CLICK, AS IF SOMEONE HAD STEPPED ON A TWIG.

(except for his microscopic bathing drawers) naked,
skipping by the lake. The angle of his legs was irresistibly
comic. The second snapshot showed Mr Bott, still short
and fat and almost naked, balancing himself on one arm

MR BOTT LEAPED AND SKIPPED AND GAMBOLLED AND
SPLASHED. HE WAS DETERMINED TO OBEY TO THE FULL
THE SPECIALIST'S ADVICE ABOUT PHYSICAL EXERCISES.

and one leg, the others stuck out wildly in the air, his eyes
staring, his tongue hanging out of his mouth. The third
snapshot showed Mr Bott in the act of overbalancing in a
rather difficult exercise. That was the gem of the collection.

The fourth showed Mr Bott lying on his back and kicking his legs in the air. The fifth showed Mr Bott standing on two very stiff arms and stiff legs with an expression of acute suffering on his face. The sixth showed Mr Bott splashing in the lake.

Mr Bott took out his handkerchief and wiped away the perspiration that was standing out on his brow.

'If you burn 'em,' said William firmly, 'we can get more. We've got the films and we can make hundreds more – and *jolly good* ones too.'

Mr Bott began to stammer.

'W-what are you g-going to d-do with them?' he asked.

'Just show them to people,' said William calmly.

Horrid visions passed before Mr Bott's eyes. He saw the wretched things in the local paper. He saw them passed from hand to hand in drawing-rooms. He saw strong men helpless with mirth as they seized on them. His position in Society – well, the less said about his position in Society if those things became public the better . . .

William took a crumpled document from his pocket and laid it solemnly upon Mr Bott's desk.

'That's a contrack,' he said, 'signed in all our life's blood sayin' that we'll keep 'em hid safely and never show 'em to anyone s'long as you let Bob stay.'

Mr Bott knew when he was beaten. He moistened his lips.

'All right,' he whispered. 'All right . . . I promise – only – *go away.*'

They went away.

Mr Bott locked the contract in his desk and pocketed the key.

Mrs Bott came in. Mr Bott still sat huddled in his chair.

'You don't look well, Botty, darling,' said Mrs Bott with concern in her voice.

'No,' said Mr Bott in a hollow voice. 'I don't know that this treatment's doing me any good.'

'Isn't it, ducky?' said Mrs Bott. 'Well, I'll try to find you a new man.'

That afternoon the Outlaws passed Bob. He stood outside his Lodge, hands in pockets, pipe in mouth, handsome, white-bearded, gloriously lazy.

'I've found a grass snake for ye, me bhoys,' he sang out. 'He's in a box in the yard beyond. Oh, an' Bob Andrews is *not* goin', me bhoys. The sack is withdrawn. Th'aud devil's realised me value, glory be to God.'

That night Robert, William's elder brother, came downstairs with his camera in his hand.

'I say,' he said, 'I could have sworn I put this away with half a dozen films in.'

'When did you have it last, dear?' said his mother.

William took a book from a shelf and sat down at the table, resting his head on his hands.

'I put it away last autumn till the decent weather came round, but I could have sworn I put it away with a roll of films in.'

His eyes fell sternly and accusingly upon William.

William looked up, met it unflinchingly with an expression of patient endurance on his face.

'Robert,' he said with a sigh. 'I wish you'd talk more quietly. I'm trying to learn my history dates.'

Robert's jaw dropped. Then he went quietly from the room still gaping. There was simply no making head or tail of that kid . . .

CHAPTER 6

'THE HAUNTED HOUSE'

'Well, you jus' tell me,' demanded William. 'You jus' give me one reason why we shun't dig for gold.'

''Cause we shan't find any,' said Douglas simply.

'How d'you know?' said William the ever-hopeful. 'How d'you know we shan't? You ever tried? You ever dug for gold? D'you know anyone what's ever dug for gold? Well, then,' triumphantly, 'how d'you *know* we shan't find any?'

'*That's* 'cause why,' said Douglas with equal triumph, ''cause no one's ever *done* it . . . 'cause they'd of done it if there'd been any chance . . .'

'They didn't think of it,' said William impatiently. 'They sim'ly didn't think of it. In the fields an' woods f'rinstance – no one can ever of dug there an' f'all you know it's *full* of gold an' jewels an' things. How can anyone *tell* till they've tried diggin'? People in England sim'ly didn't *think* of it – that's all.'

'All right,' said Douglas, tiring of the argument. 'I don't mind diggin' a bit an' tryin'.'

'You can't tell it at once – gold,' said William importantly. 'You've gotter wash it in water an' then it shows up sud'nly. So we'd better start diggin' by some water.'

They began operations the next morning by the pond, and had dug patiently for two hours before they were chased furiously from the spot by Farmer Jenks and a dog and a shower of sticks and stones. The washing of the soil had been the only part of the proceeding they had really enjoyed and a good deal of the resultant mud still adhered to their persons. They wandered down the road.

'Well, we've not found much gold yet, have we?' said Douglas sarcastically.

'D'you think the gold diggers in – in—' William's geography was rather weak, so he hastily slurred over the precise locality – 'anyway, d'you think the gold diggers found it in one morning? I bet it takes weeks an' weeks.'

'Well, 'f you think I'm goin' to go on diggin' for weeks an' weeks, I'm not!' said Douglas firmly.

'Well, where can we find some more water to dig by, anyway?' said Ginger the practical.

'It's a silly idea digging by water. I bet *I'd* see gold in the earth if there was any without washin' it,' said Henry.

'An' I bet you wun't,' said William indignantly. 'I've been readin' tales about it, an' that's what it says. D'you

112

think you're cleverer than all the gold diggers in – in – in those places?'

'Yes, I do, 'f they can't see gold without washin' it,' said Henry.

'Where's some more water, anyway?' said Ginger again plaintively.

They were passing an old house in a large garden. The house had been empty for more than a year because the last owner had died in mysterious circumstances, but that fact did not affect the Outlaws in any way. A stream flowed through the overgrown, neglected garden. William peered through the hedge.

'Water!' he called excitedly. 'Come on, an' dig for gold here.'

Led by William they scrambled through the hedge and trampled gleefully over the grass of the lawn that grew almost as high as their waists.

'Jus' like a jungle!' shouted William. 'Now we *can* imagine we're in – in – in real gold diggin' parts.'

They dug industriously for half an hour. William had a spade, 'borrowed' from the gardener. (The gardener was at that minute hunting for it through toolhouse and greenhouse and garden. His thoughts were already turning William-wards in impotent fury.) Ginger had a coal shovel with a hole in it rescued from the dustbin. Henry had a small wooden spade abstracted from his little sister when her attention was engaged elsewhere, and Douglas had a piece of wood. They threw every spadeful of earth into the stream and churned it about with their spades.

'Seems a silly idea to *me*!' objected Henry again. 'Jus' makin' *mud* of it! Seems to me you're more likely to *lose* the gold, chuckin' it into the water every time. I shun't wonder 'f we've lost lots already, sinkin' down to the bottom among the pebbles. We've not found much, anyway.'

'Well, I tell you it's the right *way*,' said William impatiently. 'It's the way they *do*. I've *read* it. If it wasn't the right way they wun't do it, would they? D'you think the gold diggers out in – out in those places would *do* it if it wasn't *right*?'

'Well, I'm gettin' a bit tired of it anyway,' said Henry.

He voiced the general opinion. Even William's enthusiasm was waning. It seemed a very hot and muddy way of getting gold . . . and it didn't even seem to get any.

Douglas had already laid aside his sodden stick and wandered up to the house. He was pressing his nose against a dirty, cracked window pane. Suddenly he shouted excitedly.

'I say . . . a *rat* . . . there's a *rat* in this room!'

The Outlaws gladly threw away their spades and

rushed to the window. There certainly was a rat. He sat upon his hind legs and trimmed his whiskers, staring at them impudently. All thought of gold left the gold diggers.

'Open the window!'

'*Catch* him!'

'Gettim! Crumbs! Gettim!'

The window actually did open. With a yell of joy William raised it and half rolled, half climbed over the sill into the room, followed by the Outlaws, uttering wild war-whoops. After one stricken glance at them the rat disappeared down his hole . . .

But the Outlaws were thrilled by the house. They tramped about the wooden floors in the empty re-echoing rooms – they slid down the dirty balusters – they found a hole in the floor and delightedly tore up all the rotten boards around it – they explored the bedrooms and the cistern loft and the filthy, airless cellars – they met four rats and chased them with deafening shouts.

They were drunk with delight. Their hands and faces were covered with dust and their hair full of cobwebs. Then William and Ginger claimed the upstairs as their castle and Henry and Douglas charged from below and they all rolled downstairs in a mass of arms and legs and cobwebs. Finally they formed a procession and marched from room to room, stamping with all their might on the wooden floors and singing lustily in their strong and inharmonious voices. They had entirely forgotten their former avocation of gold digging.

'I say,' said William at last, hot and dirty and breathless and happy, 'it'd be just the place for a meeting place, wun't it? Better than the old barn.'

'Yes, but we'd have to be quieter,' said Ginger, 'or else people'll be hearin' us an' makin' a fuss like what they always do.'

'All right!' said William sternly. 'You've been makin' more noise than anyone.'

'An' let's keep at the back,' said Henry, 'or ole Miss Hatherly'll be seein' us out of her window an' comin' in interferin'.'

William knew Miss Hatherly, whose house overlooked the front of the empty house. He had good cause to know her. Robert was deeply enamoured of Marion, Miss Hatherly's niece, and Miss Hatherly disapproved of Robert because he had no money and was still at college and rode a very noisy motorcycle and dropped cigarette ash on her carpets and never wiped his boots and frightened her canary. She disapproved of William still more and for reasons too numerous to state.

*

The empty house became the regular meeting place of the Outlaws, and the old barn was deserted. They always entered cautiously by a hole in the garden hedge, first looking up and down the road to be sure that no one saw them. The house served many purposes besides that of meeting place. It was a smugglers' den, a castle, a desert island, a battlefield, and an Indian Camp.

It was William, of course, who suggested the midnight feast and the idea was received with eager joy by the others. The next night they all got up and dressed when the rest of their households were in bed.

William climbed down the pear tree which grew right up to his bedroom window, Ginger got out of the bathroom window and crawled along the garden wall to the gate, Douglas and Henry got out of the downstairs windows. All were a-thrill with the spirit of adventure. They would not have been surprised to meet a Red Indian in full warpaint, or a smuggler with eyepatch and daggers, or a herd of lions and tigers – or even – despite their scorn of fairy tales – a witch with a cat and a broomstick walking along the moonlit road. William had brought his pistol and a good supply of caps in case they met any robbers.

'I know it wun't *kill* 'em,' he admitted, 'but the bang'd make 'em think it was a real one and scare 'em off. It

117

makes a fine bang. Not that I'm *frightened* of 'em,' he added hastily.

Ginger had brought a stick which he thought would be useful for killing snakes. He had a vague idea that all roads were infested by deadly snakes at night. They entered the house, disturbing several rats who fled at their approach.

They sat around a stubby candle-end thoughtfully provided by Henry. They ate sardines and buns and cheese and jam and cakes and dessicated coconut on the dusty floor in the empty room whose paper hung in cobwebby strands from the wall, while rats squeaked indignantly behind the wainscoting, and the moon, pale with surprise, peeped in at the dirty uncurtained window. They munched in happy silence and drank lemonade and liquorice water provided by William.

'Let's do it tomorrow, too,' said Henry as they rose to depart, and the proposal was eagerly agreed to.

Miss Hatherly was a member of the Society for the Encouragement of Higher Thought. The Society for the Encouragement of Higher Thought had exhausted nearly every branch of Higher Thought and had almost been driven to begin again at Sublimity or Relativity. (They didn't want to because, in spite of a meeting about each, they were all still doubtful as to what they meant.)

But last week someone had suggested Psychical Revelation, and they had had quite a lively meeting. Miss Sluker had a cousin whose wife thought she had heard a ghost. Miss Sluker, who was conscientious, added that the cousin's wife had never been quite sure and had admitted that it might have been a mouse. Mrs Moote had an aunt who had dreamed of her sister and the next day her sister had found a pair of spectacles which she had lost for weeks. But no one else had any psychic experience to record.

'We must have another meeting and all collect data,' said the President brightly.

'What's "data"?' said little Miss Simky to her neighbour in a mystified whisper.

'It's the French for ghost story,' said the neighbour.

'Oh!' said little Miss Simky, satisfied.

The next meeting was at Miss Hatherly's house.

The 'data' were not very extensive. Miss Euphemia Barney had discovered that her uncle had died on the same day of the month on which he had been born, but after much discussion it was decided that this, though interesting, was not a psychic experience. Miss Whatte spoke next. She said that her uncle's photograph had fallen from its hook exactly five weeks to the day after his death. They were moving the furniture, she added, and someone had just dropped the piano, but still . . . it was certainly data.

'I'm afraid I've no personal experience to record,' said little Miss Simky, 'but I've read some very exciting datas in magazines and such like, but I'm afraid they won't count.'

Then Miss Hatherly, trembling with eagerness, spoke.

'I have a very important revelation to make,' she said. 'I have discovered that Colonel Henks' old house is haunted.'

There was a breathless silence. The eyes of the members of the Society for the Encouragement of Higher Thought almost fell through their horn-rimmed spectacles on to the floor.

'*Haunted!*' they screamed in chorus, and little Miss Simky clung to her neighbour in terror.

'Listen!' said Miss Hatherly. 'The house is empty, yet I have heard voices and footsteps – the footsteps resembling Colonel Henks'. Last night,' – the round-eyed, round-mouthed circle drew nearer – 'last night I heard them most distinctly at midnight, and I firmly believe that Colonel Henks' spirit is trying to attract my attention. I believe that he has a message for me.'

Little Miss Simky gave a shrill scream and was carried to the dining-room to have hysterics in comfort among the wool mats and antimacassars.

'Tonight I shall go there,' said Miss Hatherly, and the seekers after Higher Thought screamed again.

'*Don't*, dear,' said Miss Euphemia Barney. 'Oh – it sounds so – *unsafe* – and do you think it's *quite* proper?'

'Proper?' said Miss Hatherly indignantly. 'Surely there can be no impropriety in a spirit?'

'Er – no, dear – of course, you're right,' murmured Miss Euphemia Barney, flinching under Miss Hatherly's eyes.

'I shall go tonight,' said Miss Hatherly again with one more scathing glance at Miss Euphemia Barney, 'and I shall receive the message. I want you all to meet me here this time tomorrow and I will report my experience.'

The Society for the Encouragement of Higher Thought expostulated, but finally acquiesced.

'What a *heroine*! How *brave*! How *psychic*!' they murmured as they went homewards.

'What a thrilling data it will make,' said little Miss Simky, who had now recovered from her hysterics and was feeling quite cheerful.

William was creeping downstairs. It was too windy for him to use his pear tree and he was going out by way of the dining-room window. He was dressed in an overcoat over his pyjamas and he held in his arms ten small apples which were his contribution to the feast and which he had secretly abstracted from the loft during the day. Bang! – rattle – rattle – rattle! – Three of them escaped his encircling arms and dropped noisily from stair to stair.

'Crumbs!' muttered William aghast.

No one, however, appeared to have heard. The house was still silent and sleeping. William gathered up his three apples and dropped two more in the process – fortunately upon the mat. He looked round anxiously. His arms seemed inadequate for ten apples, but he had promised ten apples for the feast and he must provide them. His pockets were already full of biscuits.

He looked round the moonlit hall. Ah, Robert's 'overflow bag'! It was on one of the chairs. Robert had been staying with a friend and had returned late that night. He had taken his suitcase upstairs and flung the small and shabby bag that he called his 'overflow bag' down on a chair. It was still there.

Good! It would do to hold the apples. William opened it. There were a few things inside, but William couldn't stay to take them out. There was plenty of room for the apples anyway. He shoved them in, took up his bag, and made his way to the dining-room window.

The midnight feast was in full swing. Henry had forgotten to bring the candles, Douglas was half asleep, Ginger was racked by gnawing internal pains as the result of the feast of the night before, and William was distrait, but otherwise all was well.

Someone had (rather misguidedly) given William a camera the day before and his thoughts were full of it. He had taken six snapshots and was going to develop them tomorrow. He had sold his bow and arrows to a classmate to buy the necessary chemicals. As he munched the apples and cheesecakes and chocolate cream and pickled onions and currants provided for the feast he was in imagination developing and fixing his snapshots. He'd never done it before. He thought he'd enjoy it. It would be so jolly and messy – watery stuff to slosh about in little basins and that kind of thing.

Suddenly, as they munched and lazily discussed the rival merits of catapults and bows and arrows (Ginger had just swopped his bow and arrows for a catapult) there came through the silent empty house the sound of the opening of the front door. The Outlaws stared at each other with crumby mouths wide open – steps were now ascending the front stairs.

'Speak!' called suddenly a loud and vibrant voice from the middle of the stairs, which made the Outlaws start almost out of their skins. 'Speak! Give me your message.'

The hair of the Outlaws stood on end.

'A ghost!' whispered Henry with chattering teeth.

'Crikey!' said William. 'Let's get out.'

They crept silently out of the further door, down the back stairs, out of the window, and fled with all their might down the road.

Meanwhile, upstairs, Miss Hatherly first walked majestically into the closed door and then fell over Robert's 'overflow bag', which the Outlaws had forgotten in their panic.

'SPEAK!' A LOUD AND VIBRANT VOICE CALLED SUDDENLY. 'SPEAK! GIVE ME YOUR MESSAGE!'

Robert went to see his beloved next day and to reassure her of his undying affection. She yawned several times in the course of his speech. She was beginning to find Robert's devotion somewhat monotonous. She was not of a constant nature. Neither was Robert.

'I say,' she said interrupting him as he was telling her for the tenth time that he had thought of her every minute

THE OUTLAWS STARED AT EACH OTHER, AND THEIR HAIR
STOOD ON END. 'A GHOST!' WHISPERED HENRY WITH
CHATTERING TEETH.

of the day, and dreamed of her every minute of the night,
and that he'd made up a lot more poetry about her but had
forgotten to bring it, 'do come indoors. They're having
some sort of stunt in the drawing-room – Aunt and the
High Thinkers, you know. I'm not quite sure what it
is – something psychic, she said, but anyway it ought to
be amusing.'

125

Rather reluctantly Robert followed her into the drawing-room where the Higher Thinkers were assembled. The Higher Thinkers looked coldly at Robert. He wasn't much thought of in high-thinking circles.

There was an air of intense excitement in the room as Miss Hatherly rose to speak.

'I entered the haunted house,' she began in a low, quivering voice, 'and at once I heard – VOICES!' Miss Simky clung in panic to Miss Sluker. 'I proceeded up the stairs and I heard – FOOTSTEPS!' Miss Euphemia Barney gave a little scream. 'I went on undaunted.'

The Higher Thinkers gave a thrilled murmur of admiration. 'And suddenly all was silent, but I felt a – PRESENCE! It led me – led me along a passage – I FELT it! It led me to a room—' Miss Simky screamed again. 'And in the room I found THIS!'

With a dramatic gesture she brought out Robert's 'overflow bag'. 'I have not yet investigated it. I wished to do so first in your presence.' ('How *noble*!' murmured Mrs Moote.) 'I feel sure that this is what Colonel Henks has been trying to show me. I am convinced that this will throw light upon the mystery of his death – I am now going to open it.'

'If it's human remains,' quavered Miss Simky, 'I shall *faint*.'

With a determined look, Miss Hatherly opened the bag. From it she brought out first a pair of faded and very much darned blue socks, next a shirt with a large hole in it, next a bathing suit, and lastly a pair of very grimy white flannel trousers.

The Higher Thinkers looked bewildered. But Miss Hatherly was not daunted.

'They're clues!' she said. 'Clues – if only we can piece them together properly; they must have some meaning. Ah, here's a notebook – this will explain everything.' She opened the notebook and began to read:

> Oh, Marion, my lady fair,
> Has eyes of blue and golden hair.
> Her heart of gold is kind and true,
> She is the sweetest girl you ever knew.
> But oh, a dragon guards this jewel
> A hideous dragon, foul and cruel,
> The ugliest old thing you ever did see,
> Is Marion's aunt Miss Hatherly.

'These socks are both marked 'Robert Brown',' suddenly squeaked Miss Sluker, who had been examining the 'clues'.

Miss Hatherly gave a scream of rage and turned to the corner where Robert had been.

127

But Robert had vanished.

When Robert saw his 'overflow bag' he had turned red.

When he saw his socks he had turned purple.

When he saw his shirt he had turned green.

When he saw his trousers he had turned white.

When he saw his notebook he had turned yellow.

When Miss Hatherly began to read he muttered something about feeling faint and crept unostentatiously out of the window. Marion followed him.

'Well,' she said sternly, 'you've made a nice mess of everything, haven't you? What on earth have you been doing?'

'I can't think what you thought of those socks,' said Robert hoarsely, 'all darned in different coloured wool, I never wear them. I don't know why they were in the bag.'

'I didn't think anything at all about them,' she snapped.

They were walking down the road towards Robert's house.

'And the shirt,' he went on in a hollow voice, 'with that big hole in it. I don't know what you'll think of my things. I just happened to have torn the shirt. I really never wear things like that.'

'Oh, do shut *up* about your things. I don't care what you wear. But I'm *sick* with you for writing soppy poetry about me for those asses to read,' she said fiercely. 'And why did you give her your bag, you loony?'

'I didn't, Marion,' said Robert miserably. 'Honestly I didn't. It's a *mystery* to me how she got it. I've been hunting for it high and low all today. It's simply a *mystery*!'

'Oh, do stop saying that. What are you going to do about it? That's the point.'

'I'm going to commit suicide,' said Robert gloomily. 'I feel there's nothing left to live for now you're turning against me.'

'I don't believe you *could*,' said Marion aggressively. 'How are you going to do it?'

'I shall drink poison.'

'What poison? I don't believe you know what poisons *are*. *What* poison?'

'Er – Prussic acid,' said Robert.

'You couldn't get it. They wouldn't sell it to you.'

'People *do* get poisons,' Robert said indignantly. 'I'm always reading of people taking poisons.'

'Well, they've got to have more sense than you,' said Marion crushingly. 'They're not the sort of people that leave their bags and soppy poems all over the place for other people to find.'

They had reached Robert's house and were standing just beneath William's window.

'I know heaps of poisons,' said Robert with dignity. 'I'm not going to tell you what I'm going to take. I'm going to—'

At that moment William, who had been (not very successfully) fixing his snapshots and was beginning to 'clear up', threw the contents of his fixing bath out of the window with a careless flourish. They fell upon Robert and Marion. For a minute they were both speechless with surprise and solution of sodium hydrosulphate. Then Marion said furiously:

'You *brute*! I hate you!'

'Oh, I *say*,' gasped Robert. 'It's not my fault, Marion. I don't know what it is. Honestly *I* didn't do it—'

Some of the solution had found its way into Robert's mouth and he was trying to eject it as politely as possible.

'It came from your beastly house,' said Marion angrily. 'And it's *ruined* my hat and I *hate* you and I'll never speak to you again.'

She turned on her heel and walked off, mopping the back of her neck with a handkerchief as she went.

Robert stared at her unrelenting back till she was out of sight, then went indoors. Ruined her hat indeed? What was a hat, anyway? It had ruined his *suit* – simply *ruined* it. And how had the old cat got his bag he'd like to know. He wouldn't mind betting a quid that that little wretch William had had something to do with it. He always had.

He decided not to commit suicide after all. He decided to live for years and years and years to make the little wretch's life a misery to him – if he could!

CHAPTER 7

WILLIAM THE MATCH-MAKER

William was feeling disillusioned. He had received, as a birthday present, a book entitled *Engineering Explained to Boys*, and had read it in bed at midnight by the light of a lamp which he had 'borrowed' from his elder brother's photographic apparatus for the purpose. The book had convinced William that it would be perfectly simple with the aid of a little machinery, to turn a wooden packing case into a motorboat. He spent two days on the work. He took all the elastic that he could find in his mother's work drawer. He disembowelled all the clockwork toys that he possessed. To supplement this he added part of the works of the morning-room clock. He completely soaked himself and his clothes in oil. Finally the thing was finished and William, stern and scowling and tousled and oily, deposited the motorboat on the edge of the pond, stepped into it and pushed off boldly. It shot into the middle of the pond and promptly sank . . . So did William. He returned home wet and muddy and oily and embittered, to meet a father who, with a grown-up's lack of sense of proportion, was waxing almost lyrical over the disappearance of the entrails of the morning-room clock.

It had been for William a thoroughly unpleasant day. He was still dwelling moodily on the memory of it.

'How was I to know the book was wrong?' he muttered indignantly as he walked down the road, his hands deep in his pockets. 'Blamin' me because the book was wrong!'

If William had not been in this mood of self-pity he would never have succumbed to the overtures of Violet Elizabeth. William at normal times disliked Violet Elizabeth. He disliked her curls and pink-and-white complexion and blue eyes and lisp and frills and flounces and imperiousness and tears. His ideal of little-girlhood was Joan, dark haired and dark eyed and shy. But Joan was away on her holidays and William's sense of grievance demanded sympathy – feminine sympathy for preference.

'Good morning, William,' said Violet Elizabeth.

'G' mornin',' said William, without discontinuing his moody scowl at the road and his hunched-up onward march.

Violet Elizabeth joined him and trotted by his side.

'You feelin' sad, William?' she said sweetly.

'Anyone'd feel sad,' burst out William. 'How was I to know a book din' know what it was talkin' about? You'd think a book'd know, wun't you? Blamin' me because a

133

book din' know what it was talkin' about! 'S'nough to make anyone feel sad! Well, you'd think a book about machinery'd know jus' a *bit* about machinery, wun't you? . . . Sinkin' me in a mucky ole pond an' then when you'd think they'd be a bit sorry for me, goin' on 's if it was *my* fault, 's if *I'd* wrote the book!'

This somewhat involved account of his wrongs seemed to satisfy Violet Elizabeth. She slipped a hand in his and for once William, the stern unbending despiser of girls, did not repel her.

'*Paw* William!' said Violet Elizabeth sweetly. 'I'm tho thorry!'

Although William kept his stern frown still fixed on the road and gave no sign of his feelings, the dulcet sympathy of Violet Elizabeth was balm to his wounded soul.

'Play gameth with me,' went on Violet Elizabeth soothingly.

William looked up and down the road. No one was in sight. After all, one must do something.

'What sort of games?' said William suspiciously, transferring his stern frown from the road to Violet Elizabeth and, contrary to his usual custom, forbearing to mimic her lisp.

'Play houth, William,' said Violet Elizabeth eagerly. 'Ith suth a nith game. You an' me be married.'

'Red Indians an' you a squaw?' said William with a gleam of interest.

'No,' said Violet Elizabeth with distaste, '*not* Red Indianth.'

'Pirates?' suggested William.

'Oh *no*, William,' said Violet Elizabeth. 'They're tho *nathty*. Juth a nordinary thort of married. You go to the offith and me go thopping and to matineeth and thee to the dinner and that thort of thing.'

William's dignity revolved from the idea.

''F you think I'd play a game like that—' he began coldly.

'Pleath do, William,' said Violet Elizabeth in a quivering voice. The blue eyes, fixed pleadingly on William, swam suddenly with tears. Violet Elizabeth exerted her sway over her immediate circle of friends and relations solely by this means. Even at that tender age she possessed the art, so indispensable to her sex, of making her blue eyes swim with tears at will. She had, on more than one occasion, found that it was the only suasion to which the stern and lordly William would yield.

He looked at her in dismay.

'All right,' he said hastily. 'All right. Come on!'

After all there was nothing else to do and one might as well do this as nothing.

Together they went into the field where was the old barn.

'Thith muth be the houth,' said Violet Elizabeth, her tears gone, her pink-and-white face wreathed in smiles. 'An' now you go to the offith, darlin' William, an' I'll thee to thingth at home. Goodbye an' work hard an' make a lot of money 'cauth I want a lot of new cloth. I've thimply nothing fit to wear. The offith ith the corner of the field. You thtay there an' count a hundred and then come back to your dinner an' bring me a box of chocolath an' a large bunch of flowerth.'

''F you *think*—' began William, hoarse with indignant surprise.

'I don' mean real oneth, William,' said Violet Elizabeth meekly. 'I mean pretend oneth. Thtickth or grath or anything'll do.'

'Or *won't*!' said William sternly. ''F you think I'm goin' even to *pretend* to give presents to an ole girl—!'

'But I'm your wife, William,' said Violet Elizabeth. There was the first stage – a suspicion of moisture – of the swimming tears in the blue eyes and William hastily retreated.

'All right, I'll *see*,' he capitulated. 'G'bye.'

'Aren't you going to kith me?' said Violet Elizabeth plaintively.

'No,' said William, 'I won't kiss you. I'm 'fraid of givin' you some sort of germ. I don't think I'd better. G'bye.'

He departed hastily for the corner of the field before the tears had time to swim. He was already regretting the rash impulse that had made him stoop to this unmanly game. He waited in the corner of the field and counted fifty. He could see Violet Elizabeth cleaning the window of the barn with a small black handkerchief, then sallying forth with languid dignified gait to interview imaginary tradespeople.

Then William suddenly espied a frog in the field beyond the hedge. He scrambled through in pursuit and captured it and spent a pleasant quarter of an hour teaching it tricks. He taught it, as he fondly imagined, to know and love him and to jump over his hands. It showed more aptitude at jumping over his hands than at knowing and loving him. It responded so well to his teaching in jumping that it finally managed to reach the ditch where it remained in discreet hiding from its late discoverer and trainer.

William then caught sight of an old nest in the hedge and went to investigate it. He decided that it must have been a robin's nest and took it to pieces to see how it was made. He came to the conclusion that he could make as good a one himself and considered the possibilities of making nests for birds during the winter and putting them ready for them in the hedges in the spring. Then he noticed that the ditch at the further end of the field was full and went there to see if he could find any water creatures. He soaked his boots and stockings, caught a newt, but, having no receptacle in which to keep it (other than his cap which seemed to hold water quite well but only for a short time) he reluctantly returned it to its native element.

Then he remembered his wife and returned slowly and not very eagerly to the barn.

Violet Elizabeth was seated in the corner of an old box in a state of majestic sulks.

'You've been at the offith for more'n a day. You've been there for monthth and yearth an' I hate you!'

'Well, I forgot all about you,' William excused himself. 'An' anyway I'd a lot of work to do at the office—'

'An' I kept waiting an' waiting and thinking you'd come back every minute and you didn't!'

'Well, how could I?' said William. 'How could I come back every minute? How could anyone come back every minute? And anyway,' as he saw Violet Elizabeth working up her all-powerful tears, 'it's lunchtime and I'm going home.'

*

William's mother was out to lunch and Ethel was her most objectionable and objecting. She objected to William's hair and to William's hands and to William's face.

'Well, I've washed 'em and I've brushed it,' said William firmly. 'I don' see what you can do more with faces an' hair than wash 'em an' brush it. 'F you don' like the colour they wash an' brush to I can't help that. It's the colour they was born with. It's their nat'ral colour. I can't do more than wash 'em an' brush it.'

'Yes, you can,' said Ethel unfeelingly. 'You can go and wash them and brush it again.'

Under the stern eye of his father who had lowered his paper for the express purpose of displaying his stern eye William had no alternative but to obey.

'Some people,' he remarked bitterly to the stair carpet as he went upstairs, 'don' care how often they make other people go up an' downstairs, tirin' themselves out. I shun't be surprised 'f I die a good lot sooner than I would have done with all this walkin' up an' downstairs tirin' myself out – an' all because my face an' hands an' hair's nat'rally a colour she doesn't like!'

Ethel was one of William's permanent grievances against Life.

But after lunch he felt cheered. He went down to the

road and there was Joan – Joan, dark eyed and dark haired and adorable – back from her holidays.

'Hello, William!' she said.

William's stern freckled countenance relaxed almost to a smile.

'Hello, Joan,' he replied.

'What you doing this afternoon, William?'

'Nothing particular,' replied William graciously.

'Let's go to the old barn and see if Ginger or any of the others are there. I'm so glad to be back, William. I hated being away. I kept thinking about you and the others and wondering what you were doing . . . you especially.'

William felt cheered and comforted. Joan generally had a soothing effect upon William.

As they neared the stile that led to the field, however, William's spirits dropped, for there, looking her most curled and cleaned and possessive, was Violet Elizabeth.

'Come on, William, and play houth again,' she called imperiously.

'Well, an' I'm not goin' to,' said William bluntly. 'An' I'm not goin' to be married to you any more an' 'f I play house I'm goin' to have Joan.'

'You can't do that,' said Violet Elizabeth calmly.

'Can't do what?'

'Can't change your wife. Ith divorth if you do an' you get hung for it.'

This nonplussed William for a moment. Then he said: 'I don' believe it. You don' know. You've never been married so you don' know anything about it.'

'I *do* know. Hereth Ginger and Douglath and Hubert Lane. You athk them.'

Ginger and Douglas and Hubert Lane, all loudly and redolently sucking Bulls' Eyes, were coming down the road. Hubert Lane was a large fat boy with protruding eyes, a superhuman appetite and a morbid love of mathematics who was only tolerated as a companion by Ginger and Douglas on account of the bag of Bulls' Eyes he carried in his pocket. He had lately much annoyed the Outlaws by haunting the field they considered theirs and, in spite of active and passive discouragement, thrusting his unwelcome comradeship upon them.

'Hi!' William hailed them loudly from the top of the stile. 'Is it divorce if you change your wife an' do you get hung for it? She says it is! 'S all *she* knows!'

The second trio gathered round the first to discuss the matter.

''S called bigamy not divorce,' said Ginger authoritatively. 'I know 'cause our cousin's gardener did it an' you get put in prison.'

141

''Th *not* big— what you said,' said Violet Elizabeth firmly. 'Ith divorth. I know 'cauth a friend of mine'th uncle did it. Tho *there*!'

The rival champions of divorce and bigamy glared at each other, and the others watched with interest.

'D'you think,' said Ginger, 'that I don' know what my own cousin's gardener did?'

'An' d'you think,' said Violet Elizabeth, 'that I don't know what my own friendth uncle did?'

'Here's Mr March comin',' said Douglas. 'Let's ask him.'

Mr March was a short stumpy young man with a very bald head and short sight. He lived in a large house at the other end of the village and rather fancied himself as a wit. He was extraordinarily conceited and not overburdened by any superfluity of intellect.

'I say, Mr March,' yelled William as he approached. 'Is it divorce or bigamy if you change your wife?'

'An' do you get hung for it or put in prison?' added Ginger.

Mr March threw back his head and roared.

'Ha, ha!' he bellowed. 'Which of you wants to change his wife? Which of you is not satisfied with his spouse? Excellent! Ha, ha!'

He went on down the road chuckling to himself.

'He's a bit cracked,' commented Ginger in a tone of kind impartiality.

'But my mother says he's awful rich,' said Douglas.

'An' he's gone on your sister,' said Ginger to William.

'Then he *mus'* be cracked!' said William bitterly.

'Anyway,' said Violet Elizabeth. 'It *ith* divorth an' I don' care if it ithn't. 'F you don' play houth with me, I'll thcream 'n' thcream till I'm thick. I can,' she added with pride.

William looked at her helplessly. 'Will you play house with me, Joan?' said Hubert, who had been fixing admiring eyes upon Joan.

'All right,' said Joan pacifically, 'and we'll live next door to you, William.'

Violet Elizabeth had gone to prepare the barn and Joan and Hubert now followed her. William glared after them fiercely.

'That ole Hubert,' he said indignantly, 'comin' messin' about in our field! I votes we chuck him out . . . jus' sim'ly chuck him out.'

'Yes,' objected Ginger, 'an' he'll tell his mother an' she'll come fussin' like what she did last time an' tellin' our fathers an' 'zaggeratin' all over the place.'

'Well, let's think of a plan, then,' said William.

Five minutes later William approached Hubert with an

'I SAY, MR MARCH,' YELLED WILLIAM,
'IS IT DIVORCE OR BIGAMY IF YOU CHANGE YOUR WIFE?'

unnatural expression of friendliness on his face. Hubert
was politely asking Violet Elizabeth to 'have a Bulls' Eye'
and Violet Elizabeth was obligingly taking three.

'I say, Hubert,' whispered William to Hubert. 'We've
gotter secret. You come over here 'n we'll tell you.'

Hubert put a Bulls' Eye into his mouth, pocketed the

'HA, HA!' LAUGHED MR MARCH. 'EXCELLENT! WHICH OF YOU IS NOT SATISFIED WITH HIS SPOUSE?'

packet and accompanied William to where Ginger and Douglas were, his goggle eyes still more a-goggle with excitement. Joan and Violet Elizabeth were busying themselves in transforming the interior of the barn into two semi-detached villas with great exercise of handkerchief-dusters and imagination.

'Douglas,' whispered William confidentially, ''s found out a secret about this field. He got it off a witch.' Hubert was so surprised that his spectacles fell off. He replaced them and listened open-mouthed.

'There's a grass in this field that if you tread on it makes you invisible. Now we're just goin' to tread about a bit to see 'f we can find it an' we don' want to leave you out of it so you can come and tread about a bit with us case we find it.'

Hubert was thrilled and flattered.

'I bet I find it first,' he squeaked excitedly.

They tramped about in silence for a few minutes. Suddenly William said in a voice of great concern:

'I say, where's Hubert gone?'

'I'm here,' said Hubert, a shade of anxiety in his voice. William looked at him and through him.

'Where's Hubert gone?' he said again. 'He was here a minute ago.'

'I'm here!' said Hubert again plaintively.

Ginger and Douglas looked first at and through Hubert and then all around the field.

'Yes, he seems to have gone,' said Ginger sadly. 'I'm 'fraid he mus' have found the grass!'

'I-I'm here!' squeaked Hubert desperately, looking rather pale.

'I'll jus' see if he's hidin' over there,' said William and proceeded literally to walk through Hubert. Hubert got the worst of the impact and sat down suddenly and heavily.

'Boo-hoo!' he wailed rising to his feet. He was promptly walked into by Ginger and sat down again with another yell.

''S mos' mysterious where he's got to,' said William. 'Let's call him!'

They yelled 'Hubert!' about the field, callously disregarding that youth's sobbing replies. Whenever he rose to his feet one of them walked through him and he sat down again with a bump and a yell.

'Did the witch say anything about makin' them visible again?' said William anxiously.

'No,' said Douglas sadly. 'I'm 'fraid he'll always be invisible now and he'll die slow of starvation 'cause no one'll ever see him to give him anything to eat.'

Hubert began to bellow unrestrainedly. He rose to his feet, dodged both Ginger and Douglas who made a dart in his direction, and ran howling towards the stile.

'Boo-hoo! I'm going home. Boo-hoo! I don' wanter die!'

As soon as he reached the stile, Ginger and Douglas and William gave a shout.

'Why, *there's* Hubert at the stile.'

Hubert ceased his tears and hung over the stile.

'Can you see me now?' he said anxiously. 'Am I all right now?'

He wiped his tears and began to clean his spectacles and straighten his collar. He was a tidy boy.

'Yes, Hubert,' said the Outlaws. 'It's all right now. We can see you now. You mus' have jus' trod on the grass. But it's all right now. Aren't you comin' back to play?'

Hubert placed one foot cautiously over the stile.

'Ginger!' said William excitedly, 'I believe he's beginning to disappear again.'

With a wild yell, Hubert turned and fled howling down the road.

'Well, we've got rid of *him*,' said William complacently, 'and if I'm not clever I don' know who *is*!'

Over-modesty was not one of William's faults.

'Well, I bet you're not quite as clever as you *think* you are,' said Ginger pugnaciously.

'How d'you know that?' said William rising to the challenge. 'How d'you know how clever I think I am? You mus' think yourself jolly clever 'f you think you know how clever I think I am!'

The discussion would have run its natural course to the physical conflict that the Outlaws found so exhilarating if Joan and Violet Elizabeth had not at this moment emerged from the barn.

'You *have* been making a noith!' said Violet Elizabeth disapprovingly. 'Wherth the boy with the Bullth Eyth?'

'Heth gonth awath,' said William unfeelingly.

'I want a Bullth Eye. You're a nathty boy to let him go away when I want a Bullth Eye.'

'Well, you can go after himth,' said William, less afraid

of her tears now that he was surrounded by his friends. But Violet Elizabeth was too angry for tears.

'Yeth and I thall!' she said. 'You're a nathty rude boy an' I don't love you and I don't want you for a huthband. I want the boy with the Bullth Eyth!'

'What about divorce or big or whatever it is?' said William, taken aback by her sudden and open repudiation of him. 'What about that? What about being hung?'

'If anyone trith to hang me,' said Violet Elizabeth complacently, 'I'll thcream and thcream and thcream till I'm thick. I can.'

Then she put out her tongue at each of the Outlaws in turn and ran lightly down the road after the figure of Hubert which could be seen in the distance.

'Well, we've got rid of *her* too,' said William, torn between relief at her departure and resentment at her scorn of him, 'and she can play her silly games with him. I've had enough of them. Let's go an' sit on the stile and see who can throw stones farthest.'

They sat in a row on the stile. It counted ten to hit the telegraph post and fifteen to reach the further edge of the opposite field.

Ethel, who had been to the village to do the household shopping, came past when the game was in full swing.

'I'll tell father,' she said grimly to William. 'He said you oughtn't to throw stones.'

William looked her up and down with his most inscrutable expression.

''F it comes to that,' he said distantly, 'he said you oughtn't to wear high heels.'

Ethel flushed angrily and walked on.

William's spirits rose. It wasn't often he scored over Ethel and he feared that even now she would have her revenge.

He watched her go down the road. Coming back along the road was Mr March. As he met Ethel a deep flush and a sickly smile overspread his face. He stopped and spoke to her, gazing at her with a sheep-like air. Ethel passed on haughtily. He had recovered slightly when he reached the Outlaws, though traces of his flush still remained.

'Well,' he said with a loud laugh. 'Divorce or bigamy? Which is it to be? Ha, ha! Excellent!'

He put his walking stick against Ginger's middle and playfully pushed him off the stile backwards. Then he went on his way laughing loudly.

'I said he was cracked!' said Ginger climbing back to his perch.

'He'd jus' about suit Ethel then,' said William bitterly.

They sat in silence a few minutes. There was a faraway meditative look in William's eyes.

'I say,' he said at last, ''f Ethel married him she'd go away from our house and live in his, wun't she?'

'U-hum,' agreed Ginger absently as he tried to hit the second tree to the left of the telegraph post that counted five.

'I wish there was some way of makin' them fall in love with each other,' said William gloomily.

'Oh, there is, William,' said Joan. 'We've been learning it at school. Someone called Shakespeare wrote it. You keep saying to both of them that the other's in love with them and they fall in love and marry. I know. We did it last term. One of them was Beatrice and I forget the other.'

'You said it was Shakespeare,' said William.

'No, he's the one that tells about it.'

'Sounds a queer sort of tale to me,' said William severely. 'Couldn't you write to him and get it a bit plainer what to do?'

'Write to him!' jeered Ginger. 'He's dead. Fancy you not knowin' that! Fancy you not knowin' Shakespeare's dead!'

'Well, how was I to know he was dead? I can't know everyone's name what's dead, can I? I bet there's lots of dead folks' names what you don' know!'

'Oh, do you?' said Ginger. 'Well, I bet I know more dead folks' names than you do!'

'He said that anyway,' interposed Joan hastily and

pacifically. 'He said that if you keep on making up nice things and saying that the other said it about them they fall in love and marry. It must be true because it's in a book.'

There was a look of set purpose in William's eyes.

'It'll take a bit of arrangin',' was the final result of his frowning meditation, 'but it might come off all right.'

William's part was more difficult than Joan's. William's part consisted in repeating to Ethel compliments supposed to emanate from Mr March. If Ethel had had the patience to listen to them she would have realised that they all bore the unmistakable imprint of William's imagination.

William opened his campaign by approaching her when she was reading a book in the drawing-room.

'I say, Ethel,' he began in a deep soulful voice, 'I saw Mr March this afternoon.'

Ethel went on reading as if she had not heard.

'He says,' continued William mournfully, sitting on the settee next to Ethel, 'he says that you're the apple of his life. He says that he loves you with a mos' devourin' passion. He says that you're ab's'lutely the mos' beauteous maid he's ever come across.'

'Be quiet and let me read!' said Ethel without looking up from her book.

'He says,' went on William in the same deep monotonous voice, 'he says that he doesn't mind your hair bein' red though he knows some people think it's ugly. That's noble of him, you know, Ethel. He says—'

Ethel rose from the settee.

'If you won't be quiet,' she said, 'I'll have to go into another room.'

She went into the dining-room and, sitting down in an armchair, began to read again.

After a short interval William followed and taking the armchair opposite hers, continued:

'He says, Ethel, that he's deep in love with you and that he doesn't mind you bein' so bad-tempered. He likes it. Anyway he 'spects he'll get used to it. He says he adores you jus' like what people do on the pictures. He puts his hand on his stomach and rolls his eyes whenever he thinks of you. He says—'

'Will – you – be – quiet?' said Ethel angrily.

'No, but jus' listen, Ethel,' pleaded William. 'He says—'

Ethel flounced out of the room. She went to the morning-room, locked the door, and, sitting down with her back to the window, continued to read. After a few minutes came the sound of the windows being cautiously opened and William appeared behind her chair.

'I say, Ethel, when I saw Mr March he said—'

Ethel gave a scream.

'If you mention that man's name to me once more, William, I'll – I'll tell Father that you've been eating the grapes in the hothouse.'

It was a random shot but with a boy of William's many activities such random shots generally found their mark.

He sighed and slowly retreated from the room by way of the window.

Ethel's attitude made his task a very difficult one . . .

Joan's task was easier. Joan had free access to her father's study and typewriter and Joan composed letters from Ethel to Mr March. William 'borrowed' some of his father's notepaper for her and she worked very conscientiously, looking up the spelling of every word in the dictionary and re-typing every letter in which she made a mistake. She sent him one every day. Each one ended, 'Please do not answer this or mention it to me and do not mind if my manner to you seems different to these letters. I cannot explain, but you know that my heart is full of love for you.'

One letter had a PS: 'I would be grateful if you would give half a crown to my little brother William when next you meet him. I am penniless and he is such a nice good boy.'

Anyone less conceited than Mr March would have suspected the genuineness of the letters, but to Mr March they seemed just such letters as a young girl who had succumbed to his incomparable charm might write.

It was William who insisted on the PS though Joan felt that it was inartistic. It had effect, however. Mr March met William on the road the next morning and handed him a half-crown, then with a loud guffaw and 'Divorce or bigamy, eh?' pushed William lightly into a holly bush and passed on. Mr March's methods of endearing himself to the young were primitive . . . But the half-crown compensated for the holly bush in William's estimation. He wanted to make the PS a regular appendage to the letter but Joan firmly refused to allow it.

After a week of daily letters written by Joan and daily unsuccessful attempts on the part of William to introduce imaginary compliments from Mr March into casual conversation with Ethel, both felt that it was time for the dénouement.

The final letter was the result of a hard morning's work by William and Joan.

Dear George (May I call you George now?),
Will you meet me by the river near Fisher's Lock tomorrow afternoon at three o'clock? Will you wear a red

carnation and I will wear a red rose as gages of our love? I want to tell you how much I love you, though I am sure you know. Let us be married next Monday afternoon. Do not speak to me of this letter but just come wearing a red carnation and I will come wearing a red rose as gages of our love. I hope you will love my little brother William too. He is very fond of caramels.

Yours with love,
ETHEL BROWN (soon I hope to be March).

The reference to William had been the subject of much discussion, but William had overborne Joan's objections.

'I reely only want it put because it makes it seem more nat'ral. It's only nat'ral she should want him to be kind to her brother. I mean, not knowin' Ethel as well as I do, he'll *think* it nat'ral.'

The stage managing of the actual encounter was the most difficult part of all. Ethel's reception of her swain's supposed compliments had not been such as to make William feel that a request to meet him at Fisher's Lock would be favourably received. He was feeling a little doubtful about the working of Joan's love charm in the case of Ethel, but with his usual optimism he was hoping for the best.

'Ethel,' he said at lunch, 'Gladys Barker wants to see you this afternoon. I met her this morning.'

'Did she say any time?' said Ethel.

'Soon after three,' said William.

'Why on earth didn't you tell me sooner?' said Ethel.

The road to Gladys Barker's house lay by the river past Fisher's Lock.

''S not tellin' a story,' William informed his conscience. 'I did meet her this mornin' an' I don' know that she doesn't want to see Ethel this afternoon. She prob'ly does.'

About quarter to three William came in from the garden carefully holding a rose. He wore his most inscrutable expression.

'I thought you might like to wear this, Ethel,' he said. 'It goes nice with your dress.'

Ethel was touched.

'Thank you, William,' she said.

She watched him as he returned to the garden, humming discordantly.

She wondered if sometimes she misjudged William . . .

It was ten minutes past three. On the path by the river near Fisher's Lock stood Mr March with a red carnation in his buttonhole. Concealed in a tree just above his head were Ginger, Douglas, William and Joan.

157

Down the path by the river came Ethel wearing her red rose.

Mr March started forward.

'Well, little girl?' he said with roguish tenderness.

Ethel stopped suddenly and stared at him in amazement.

'Ah!' said Mr March, shaking a fat finger at her. 'The time has come to drop the mask of haughtiness. I know all now, you know, from your own sweet lips, I mean your own sweet pen . . . I know how your little heart beats at the thought of your George. I know who is your ideal . . . your beloved knight . . . your all those sweet things you wrote to me. Now, don't be frightened, little girl. I return your affection, but not Monday afternoon! I don't think we can manage it quite as soon as that.'

'Mr March,' said Ethel, 'are you ill?'

'Ill, my little precious?' ogled Mr March. 'No, well, my little popsie! Your dear loving letters have made me well. I was so touched by them, little Ethelkins! . . . You thinking me so handsome and clever and, you know, I admire you too.' He touched the red rose she was wearing playfully. 'The gage of your love, eh?'

'Mr March,' said Ethel angrily, 'you must be mad. I've never written to you in my life.'

'Ah,' he replied, 'do not deny the fond impeachment.'

'NOW, DON'T BE FRIGHTENED, LITTLE GIRL,'
SAID MR MARCH. 'I KNOW HOW YOUR LITTLE HEART
BEATS AT THE THOUGHT OF YOUR GEORGE.'
'MR MARCH!' EXCLAIMED ETHEL, 'ARE YOU ILL?'

He took a bundle of typewritten letters out of his pocket and handed them to her. 'You have seen these before.'

She took them and read them slowly one by one.

'I've never heard such rubbish,' she said at last. 'I've never seen the idiotic things before. You must be crazy.'

Mr March's mouth fell open.

'You – didn't write them?' he said incredulously.

'Of course not!' snapped Ethel. 'How could you be such a fool as to think I did?'

He considered for a minute, then his expression of bewilderment gave place again to the roguish smile.

'Ah, naughty!' he said. 'She's being very coy! I know better! I know—'

He took her hand. Ethel snatched it back and pushed him away angrily. He was standing on the very edge of the river and at the push he swayed for a second, clutching wildly at the air, then fell with a loud splash into the stream.

'Oh, I say, Ethel,' expostulated William from his leafy hiding place. 'Don't carry on like that . . . drownin' him after all the trouble we've took with him! He's gotter lot of money an' a nice garden an' a big house. Anyone'd think you'd want to marry him 'stead of carryin' on like that!'

At the first sound of his voice, Ethel had gazed round

open-mouthed, then she looked up into the tree and saw William.

'You *hateful* boy!' she cried. 'I'm going straight home to tell Father!'

She turned on her heel and went off without looking back.

Meanwhile Mr March was scrambling up the bank, spitting out water and river weeds and (fortunately) inarticulate expletives.

'I'll have damages off someone for this!' he said as he emerged on to the bank. 'I'll make someone pay for this! I'll have the law on them! I'll . . .'

He went off dripping and muttering and shaking his fist vaguely in all directions . . .

Slowly the Outlaws climbed down from their tree.

'Well, you've made a nice mess of everything!' said Ginger dispassionately.

'I've took a lot of trouble trying to get her married,' said William, 'and this is how she pays me! Well, she needn't blame me.' He looked at the indignant figure of his pretty nineteen-year-old sister which was still visible in the distance and added gloomily: 'She's turnin' out an old maid an' it's not my fault. I've done my best. Seems to me she's goin' to go on livin' in our house all her life till she dies, an' that's a nice look out for me, isn't it? Seems to me that if she won't even get married when you practically fix it all up for her an' save her all the trouble like this, she won't *ever* marry an' she needn't blame me 'cause she's an old maid. I've done everythin' I can. An' you,' he transferred his stern eye to Joan. 'Why don' you read books with a bit of *sense* in them? This Shake man simply doesn't know what he's talkin' about. It's a good thing for him he *is* dead, gettin' us all into a mess like this!'

'What are you goin' to do now?' said Douglas with interest.

'I'm goin' fishin',' said William, 'an' I don' care if I don't get home till bedtime.'

It was a week later. The excitement and altercations and retaliations and dealing out of justice which had followed William's abortive attempt to marry Ethel were over.

Ethel had gone into the morning-room for a book. The Outlaws were playing in the garden outside. Their strong young voices floated in through the open window.

'Now let's have a change,' William was saying. 'Ginger be Mr March an' Joan be Ethel . . . Now, begin . . . go on . . . Joan, come on . . . walkin' kind of silly like Ethel . . . an' Ginger go to meet her with a soft look on your face . . . That's it . . . now, start!'

'Well, little girl?' said Ginger in a shrill affected voice.

'I know how your little heart beats at me. I know I am your knight an' all that.'

'You've left a lot out,' said William. 'You've left out where he said he wouldn't marry her on Monday. Now you go on, Joan.'

'Mr March,' squeaked Joan in piercing hauteur, 'are you mad?'

'No,' corrected William. '"Are you feelin' ill?" comes first. Let's start again an' get it all right . . .'

Ethel flounced out of the room and slammed the door. She found her mother in the dining-room darning socks.

'Mother,' she said, 'can't we *do* anything about William? Can't we send him to an orphanage or anything?'

'No, darling,' said Mrs Brown calmly. 'You see, for one thing, he isn't an orphan.'

'But he's so *awful*!' said Ethel. 'He's so unspeakably dreadful!'

'Oh, no, Ethel,' said Mrs Brown still darning placidly. 'Don't say things like that about your little brother. I sometimes think that when William's just had his hair cut and got a new suit on, he looks quite sweet!'

CHAPTER 8

WILLIAM'S TRUTHFUL CHRISTMAS

William went to church with his family every Sunday morning but he did not usually listen to the sermon. He considered it a waste of time. He sometimes enjoyed singing the psalms and hymns. Any stone-deaf person could have told when William was singing the psalms and hymns by the expressions of pain on the faces of those around him. William's singing was loud and discordant. It completely drowned the organ and the choir. Miss Barney, who stood just in front of him, said that it always gave her a headache for the rest of the week. William contested with some indignation that he had as good a right to sing in church as anyone. Besides, there was nothing wrong with his voice . . . It was just like everyone else's . . .

During the Vicar's sermon, William either stared at the curate (William always scored in this game because the curate invariably began to grow pink and look embarrassed after about five minutes of William's stare) or held a face-pulling competition with the red-haired choir boy or amused himself with insects, conveyed to church in a matchbox in his pocket, till restrained by the united glares of his father and mother and Ethel and Robert . . .

But this Sunday, attracted by the frequent repetition of the word 'Christmas', William put his stag beetle back into its box and gave his whole attention to the Vicar's exhortation . . .

'What is it that poisons our whole social life?' said the Vicar earnestly. 'What is it that spoils even the holy season that lies before us? It is deceit. It is untruthfulness. Let each one of us decide here and now for this season of Christmas at least, to cast aside all deceit and hypocrisy and speak the truth one with another . . . It will be the first step to a holier life. It will make this Christmas the happiest of our lives . . .'

William's attention was drawn from the exhortation by the discovery that he had not quite closed the matchbox and the stag beetle was crawling up Ethel's coat. Fortunately Ethel was busily engaged in taking in all the details of Marion Hatherly's new dress across the aisle and did not notice. William recaptured his pet and shut up the matchbox . . . then rose to join lustily and inharmoniously in the first verse of 'Onward, Christian Soldiers'. During the other verses he employed himself by trying a perfectly new grimace (which he had been practising all week) on the choir boy. It was intercepted by the curate who shuddered and looked away hastily. The sight and sound of William in the second row from the front completely spoilt the service for the curate every Sunday. He was an aesthetic young man and William's appearance and personality hurt his sense of beauty . . .

But the words of the sermon had made a deep impression on William. He decided for this holy season at least to cast aside deceit and hypocrisy and speak the truth one with another . . . William had not been entirely without aspiration to a higher life before this. He had once decided to be self-sacrificing for a whole day and his efforts had been totally unappreciated and misunderstood. He had once tried to reform others and the result had been even more disastrous. But he'd never made a real effort to cast aside deceit and hypocrisy and to speak the truth one with another. He decided to try it at Christmas as the Vicar had suggested.

Much to his disgust William heard that Uncle Frederick and Aunt Emma had asked his family to stay with them for Christmas. He gathered that the only drawback to the arrangement in the eyes of his family was himself, and the probable effect of his personality on the peaceful household of Uncle Frederick and Aunt Emma. He was not at all offended. He was quite used to this view of himself.

'All right!' he said obligingly. 'You jus' go. I don' mind. I'll stay at home . . . you jus' leave me money an' my presents an' I won't mind a bit.'

William's spirits in fact soared sky-high at the prospect of such an oasis of freedom in the desert of parental interference. But his family betrayed again that strange disinclination to leave William to his own devices that hampered so many of William's activities.

'No, William,' said his mother, 'we certainly can't do that. You'll have to come with us but I do hope you'll be good.'

William remembered the sermon and his good resolution.

'Well,' he said cryptically, 'I guess 'f you knew what I was goin' to be like at Christmas you'd almost *want* me to come.'

It happened that William's father was summoned on Christmas Eve to the sickbed of one of his aunts and so could not accompany them, but they set off under Robert's leadership and arrived safely.

Uncle Frederick and Aunt Emma were very stout and good-natured-looking, but Uncle Frederick was the stouter and more good-natured-looking of the two. They had not seen William since he was a baby. That explained the fact of their having invited William and his family to spend Christmas with them. They lived too far away to have heard even rumours of the horror with which William inspired the grown-up world around him. They greeted William kindly.

'So this is little William,' said Uncle Frederick, putting his hand on William's head. 'And how is little William?'

William removed his head from Uncle Frederick's hand in silence then said distantly:

'V' well, thank you.'

'And so grateful to your Uncle and Aunt for asking you to stay with them, aren't you, William?' went on his mother.

William remembered that his career of truthfulness did not begin till the next day so he said still more distantly: 'Yes.'

That evening Ethel said to her mother in William's presence:

'Well, he's not been so *bad* today, considering.'

'You wait,' said William unctuously. 'You wait till tomorrow when I start castin' aside deceit an' . . . an'— Today'll be *nothin'* to it.'

William awoke early on Christmas day. He had hung up his stocking the night before and was pleased to see it fairly full. He took out the presents quickly but not very optimistically. He had been early disillusioned in the matter of grown-ups' capacity for choosing suitable presents. Memories of prayer books and history books and socks and handkerchiefs floated before his mental vision . . . Yes, as bad as ever! . . . A case containing a pen and pencil and ruler, a new brush and comb, a purse (empty) and a new tie . . . a penknife and a box of toffee were the only redeeming features. On the chair by his bedside was a book of Church History from Aunt Emma and a box containing a pair of compasses, a protractor and a set square from Uncle Frederick . . .

William dressed, but as it was too early to go down he sat down on the floor and ate all his tin of toffee. Then he turned his attention to his Church History book. He read a few pages but the character and deeds of the saintly Aidan so exasperated him that he was driven to relieve his feeling by taking his new pencil from its case and adorning the saint's picture by the addition of a top hat and spectacles. He completed the alterations by a moustache and by changing the book the saint held into an attaché case. He made similar alterations to every picture in the book . . . St Oswald seemed much improved by them and this cheered William considerably. Then he took his penknife and began to carve his initials upon his brush and comb . . .

*

William appeared at breakfast wearing his new tie and having brushed his hair with his new brush or rather with what was left of his new brush after his very drastic initial-carving. He carried under his arm his presents for his host and hostess. He exchanged 'Happy Christmas' gloomily. His resolve to cast away deceit and hypocrisy and speak the truth one with another lay heavy upon him. He regarded it as an obligation that could not be shirked. William was a boy of great tenacity of purpose. Having once made up his mind to a course, he pursued it regardless of consequences . . .

'Well, William, darling,' said his mother, 'did you find your presents?'

'Yes,' said William gloomily. 'Thank you.'

'Did you like the book and instruments that Uncle and I gave you?' said Aunt Emma brightly.

'No,' said William gloomily and truthfully. 'I'm not int'rested in Church History an' I've got something like those at school. Not that I'd want 'em,' he added hastily, 'if I hadn't 'em.'

'*William!*' screamed Mrs Brown in horror. 'How can you be so ungrateful?'

'I'm not ungrateful,' explained William wearily. 'I'm only bein' truthful. I'm casting aside deceit an' . . . an' hyp-hyp-what he said. I'm only sayin' that I'm not int'rested in Church History nor in those inst'ments. But thank you very much for 'em.'

There was a gasp of dismay and a horrified silence during which William drew his paper packages from under his arm.

'Here are your Christmas presents from me,' he said.

The atmosphere brightened. They unfastened their parcels with expressions of anticipation and Christian forgiveness upon their faces. William watched them, his face 'registering' only patient suffering.

'It's very kind of you,' said Aunt Emma still struggling with the string.

'It's not kind,' said William still treading doggedly the path of truth. 'Mother said I'd got to bring you something.'

Mrs Brown coughed suddenly and loudly but not in time to drown the fatal words of truth . . .

'But still – er – very kind,' said Aunt Emma though with less enthusiasm.

At last she brought out a small pincushion.

'Thank you very much, William,' she said. 'You really oughtn't to have spent your money on me like this.'

'I din't,' said William stonily. 'I hadn't any money, but I'm very glad you like it. It was left over from Mother's stall at the Sale of Work, an' Mother said it

171

was no use keepin' it for nex' year because it had got so faded.'

Again Mrs Brown coughed loudly but too late. Aunt Emma said coldly:

'I see. Yes. Your mother was quite right. But thank you all the same, William.'

Uncle Frederick had now taken the wrappings from his present and held up a leather purse.

'Ah, this is a really useful present,' he said jovially.

'I'm 'fraid it's not very useful,' said William. 'Uncle Jim sent it to Father for his birthday but Father said it was no use 'cause the catch wouldn' catch so he gave it to me to give to you.'

Uncle Frederick tried the catch.

'Um . . . ah . . .' he said. 'Your father was quite right. The catch won't catch. Never mind, I'll send it back to your father as ˋ⌣ ⌣ present . . . what?'

As soon as the Brown family were left alone it turned upon William in a combined attack.

'I *warned* you!' said Ethel to her mother.

'He ought to be hung,' said Robert.

'William, how *could* you?' said Mrs Brown.

'When I'm bad, you go on at me,' said William with exasperation, 'an' when I'm tryin' to lead a holier life and cast aside hyp – hyp – what he said, you go on at me. I dunno what I *can* be. I don't mind bein' hung. I'd as soon be hung as keep havin' Christmas over an' over again simply every year the way we do . . .'

William accompanied the party to church after breakfast. He was slightly cheered by discovering a choir boy with a natural aptitude for grimaces and an instinctive knowledge of the rules of the game. The Vicar preached an unconvincing sermon on unselfishness and the curate gave full play to an ultra-Oxford accent and a voice that was almost as unmusical as William's. Aunt Emma said it had been a 'beautiful service'. The only bright spot to William was when the organist boxed the ears of the youngest choir boy, who retaliated by putting out his tongue at the organist at the beginning of each verse of the last hymn . . .

William was very silent during lunch . . . He simply didn't know what people saw in Christmas. It was just like ten Sundays rolled into one . . . An' they didn't even give people the sort of presents they'd like . . . No one all his life had ever given him a water pistol or a catapult or a trumpet or bows and arrows or anything really useful . . . And if they didn't like truth an' castin' aside deceit an' – an' the other thing they could do without . . . but he was jolly well goin' to go on with it. He'd made up his mind and he was jolly well goin' to go on with it . . .

His silence was greatly welcomed by his family. He ate plentifully, however, of the turkey and plum pudding and felt strangely depressed afterwards . . . so much that he followed the example of the rest of the family and went up to his bedroom . . .

There he brushed his hair with his new brush, but he had carved his initials so deeply and spaciously that the brush came in two with the first flourish. He brushed his shoes with the two halves with great gusto in the manner of the professional shoeblack . . . Then having nothing else to do, he turned to his Church History again. The desecrated pictures of the saints met his gaze and realising suddenly the enormity of the crime in grown-up eyes he took his penknife and cut them all out. He made paper boats of them, and deliberately and because he hated it he cut his new tie into strips to fasten some of the boats together. He organised a thrilling naval battle with them and was almost forgetting his grudge against life in general and Christmas in particular . . .

He was roused to the sense of the present by sounds of life and movement downstairs, and, thrusting his saintly paper fleet into his pyjama case, he went down to the drawing-room. As he entered there came the sound of a car drawing up at the front door and Uncle Frederick looked out of the window and groaned aloud.

'It's Lady Atkinson,' he said. 'Help! Help!'

'Now, Frederick, dear,' said Aunt Emma hastily. 'Don't talk like that and *do* try to be nice to her. She's one of *the* Atkinson's, you know,' she explained with empressement to Mrs Brown in a whisper as the lady was shown in.

Lady Atkinson was stout and elderly and wore a very youthful hat and coat.

'A happy Christmas to you all!' she said graciously. 'The boy? Your nephew? William? How do you do, William? He – *stares* rather, doesn't he? Ah, yes,' she greeted everyone separately with infinite condescension.

'I've brought you my Christmas present in person,' she went on in the tone of voice of one giving an unheard-of-treat. 'Look!'

She took out of an envelope a large signed photograph of herself. 'There now . . . what do you think of that?'

Murmurs of surprise and admiration and gratitude.

Lady Atkinson drank them in complacently.

'It's very good, isn't it? You . . . little boy . . . don't you think it's very like me?'

William gazed at it critically.

'It's not as fat as you are,' was his final offering at the altar of truth.

'*William!*' screamed Mrs Brown, 'how *can* you be so impolite?'

175

'Impolite?' said William with some indignation. 'I'm not tryin' to be polite! I'm bein' truthful. I can't be everything. Seems to me I'm the only person in the world what *is* truthful an' no one seems to be grateful to me. It *isn't* 's fat as what she is,' he went on doggedly, 'an' it's not got as many little lines on its face as what she has an' it's different-lookin' altogether. It looks pretty an' she doesn't—'

Lady Atkinson towered over him, quivering with rage.

'You *nasty* little boy!' she said thrusting her face close to his. 'You – NASTY – little – boy!'

Then she swept out of the room without another word.

The front door slammed.

She was gone.

Aunt Emma sat down and began to weep.

'She'll never come to the house again,' she said.

'I always said he ought to be hung,' said Robert gloomily. 'Every day we let him live he complicates our lives still worse.'

'I shall tell your father, William,' said Mrs Brown, '*directly* we get home.'

'The kindest thing to think,' said Ethel, 'is that he's mad.'

'Well,' said William, 'I don' know what I've done 'cept cast aside deceit an' – an' the other thing what he said in church an' speak the truth an' that. I don' know why

'DON'T YOU THINK IT'S VERY LIKE ME?'
ASKED LADY ATKINSON.
'IT'S NOT AS FAT AS YOU ARE,' SAID WILLIAM CRITICALLY.
'I'M NOT IMPOLITE. I'M BEING TRUTHFUL.'

everyone's so mad at me jus' 'cause of that. You'd think they'd be glad!'

'She'll never set foot in the house again,' sobbed Aunt Emma.

Uncle Frederick, who had been vainly trying to hide his glee, rose.

'I don't think she will, my dear,' he said cheerfully. 'Nothing like the truth, William . . . absolutely nothing.'

He pressed a half-crown into William's hand surreptitiously as he went to the door . . .

A diversion was mercifully caused at this moment by the arrival of the post. Among it there was a Christmas card from an artist who had a studio about five minutes' walk from the house. This little attention comforted Aunt Emma very much.

'How kind of him!' she said. 'And we never sent him anything. But there's that calendar that Mr Franks sent to us and it's not written on. Perhaps William could be trusted to take it to Mr Fairly with our compliments while the rest of us go for a short walk.' She looked at William rather coldly.

William, who was feeling the atmosphere indoors inexplicably hostile (except for Uncle Frederick's equally inexplicable friendliness), was glad of an excuse for escaping.

He set off with the calendar wrapped in brown paper. On the way his outlook on life was considerably brightened by finding a street urchins' fight in full swing. He joined in with gusto and was soon acclaimed leader of his side. This exhilarating adventure was ended by a policeman, who scattered the combatants and pretended to chase William down a side street in order to vary the monotony of his Christmas 'beat'.

William, looking rather battered and dishevelled, arrived at Mr Fairly's studio. The calendar had fortunately survived the battle unscathed and William handed it to Mr Fairly who opened the door. Mr Fairly showed him into the studio with a low bow. Mr Fairly was clothed in correct artistic style . . . baggy trousers, velvet coat and a flowing tie. He had a pointed beard and a theatrical manner. He had obviously lunched well – as far as liquid refreshment was concerned at any rate. He was moved to tears by the calendar.

'How kind! How very kind . . . My dear young friend, forgive this emotion. The world is hard. I am not used to kindness. It unmans me . . .'

He wiped away his tears with a large mauve and yellow handkerchief. William gazed at it fascinated.

'If you will excuse me, my dear young friend,' went on Mr Fairly, 'I will retire to my bedroom where I have the wherewithal to write and indite a letter of thanks to your most delightful and charming relative. I beg you to make yourself at home here . . . Use my house, my dear young friend, as though it were your own . . .'

He waved his arms and retreated unsteadily to an inner room, closing the door behind him.

William sat down on a chair and waited. Time passed, William became bored. Suddenly a fresh aspect of his Christmas resolution occurred to him. If you were speaking the truth one with another yourself, surely you might take everything that other people said for truth . . . He'd said, 'Use this house, my dear young friend, as though it were your own . . .' Well, he would. The man prob'ly meant it . . . well, anyway, he shouldn't have said it if he didn't . . . William went across the room and opened a cupboard. It contained a medley of paints, two palettes, two oranges and a cake. The feeling of oppression that had followed William's Christmas lunch had faded and he attacked the cake with gusto. It took about ten minutes to finish the cake and about four to finish the oranges. William felt refreshed. He looked round the studio with renewed interest. A lay figure sat upon a couch on a small platform. William approached it cautiously. It was almost life-size and clad in a piece of thin silk. William lifted it. It was quite light. He put it on a chair by the window. Then he went to the little back room. A bonnet and mackintosh (belonging to Mr Fairly's charwoman) hung there. He dressed the lay figure in the bonnet and mackintosh. He found a piece of black gauze in a drawer and put it over the figure's face as a veil and tied it round the bonnet. He felt all the thrill of the creative artist. He shook hands with it and talked to it. He began to have a feeling of deep affection for it. He called it Annabel. The clock struck and he remembered the note he was waiting for . . . He knocked gently at the bedroom door. There was no answer. He opened the door and entered. On the writing-table by the door was a letter:

Dear Friend,
Many thanks for your beautiful calendar. Words fail me . . .

Then came a blot – mingled ink and emotion – and that was all. Words had failed Mr Fairly so completely that he lay outstretched on the sofa by the window sleeping the sleep of the slightly inebriated. William thought he'd better not wake him up. He returned to the studio and carried on his self-imposed task of investigation. He found some acid drops in a drawer adhering to a tube of yellow ochre. He separated them and ate the acid drops but their strong flavour of yellow ochre made him feel sick and he returned to Annabel for sympathy . . .

Then he thought of a game. The lay figure was a captured princess and William was the gallant rescuer. He went outside, opened the front door cautiously, crept into the hall, hid behind the door, dashed into the studio, caught up the figure in his arms and dashed into the street with it. The danger and exhilaration of a race for freedom through the streets with Annabel in his arms was too enticing to be resisted. As a matter of fact the flight through the streets was rather disappointing. He met no one and no one pursued him . . .

He staggered up the steps to Aunt Emma's house still carrying Annabel. There, considering the matter for the first time in cold blood, he realised that his rescue of Annabel was not likely to be received enthusiastically by his home circle. And Annabel was not easy to conceal. The house seemed empty but he could already hear its inmates returning from their walk. He felt a sudden hatred of Annabel for being so large and unhideable. He could not reach the top of the stairs before they came in at the door. The drawing-room door was open and into it he rushed, deposited Annabel in a chair by the fireplace with her back to the room, and returned to the hall. He smoothed back his hair, assumed his most vacant expression and awaited them. To his surprise they crept past the drawing-room door on tiptoe and congregated in the dining-room.

'A caller,' said Aunt Emma. 'Did you see?'

'Yes, in the dining-room,' said Mrs Brown. 'I saw her hat through the window.'

'Curse!' said Uncle Frederick.

'The maids must have shown her in before they went up to change. I'm simply *not* going to see her. On Christmas day, too! I'll just wait till she gets tired and goes or till one of the maids comes down and can send her away!'

'Shh!' said Uncle Frederick. 'She'll hear you.'

Aunt Emma lowered her voice.

'I don't think she's a lady,' she said. 'She didn't look it through the window.'

'Perhaps she's collecting for something,' said Mrs Brown.

'Well,' said Aunt Emma sinking her voice to a conspiratorial whisper, 'if we stay in here and keep very quiet she'll get tired of waiting and go.'

William was torn between an interested desire to be safely out of the way when the dénouement took place and a disinterested desire to witness the dénouement. The latter won and he stood at the back of the group with a sphinx-like expression upon his freckled face . . .

They waited in silence for some minutes then Aunt

183

Emma said: 'Well, she'll stay for ever it seems to me if someone doesn't send her away. Frederick, go and turn her out.'

They all crept into the hall. Uncle Frederick went just inside and coughed loudly. Annabel did not move. Uncle Frederick came back.

'Deaf!' he whispered. 'Stone deaf! Someone else try.'

Ethel advanced boldly into the middle of the room. 'Good afternoon,' she said clearly and sweetly.

Annabel did not move. Ethel returned.

'I think she must be asleep,' said Ethel.

'She looks drunk to me,' said Aunt Emma, peeping round the door.

'I shouldn't wonder if she was dead,' said Robert. 'It's just the sort of thing you read about in books. Mysterious dead body found in drawing-room. I bet I can find a few clues to the murder if she is dead.'

'*Robert!*' reproved Mrs Brown in a shrill whisper.

'Perhaps you'd better fetch the police, Frederick,' said Aunt Emma.

'I'll have one more try,' said Uncle Frederick.

He entered the room.

'Good afternoon,' he bellowed.

Annabel did not move. He went up to her.

'Now look here, my woman—' he began, laying his hand on her shoulder . . .

Then the dénouement happened.

Mr Fairly burst into the house like a whirlwind still slightly inebriated and screaming with rage.

'Where's the thief? Where is he? He's stolen my figure. He's eaten my tea. I shall have to eat my supper for my tea and my breakfast for my supper . . . I shall be a meal wrong always . . . I shall never get right. And it's all his fault. Where is he? He's stolen my charwoman's clothes. He's stolen my figure. He's eaten my tea. Wait till I get him!' He caught sight of Annabel, rushed into the drawing-room, caught her up in his arms and turned round upon the circle of open-mouthed spectators. 'I *hate* you!' he screamed. 'And your nasty little calendars and your nasty little boys! Stealing my figure and eating my tea . . . I'll light the fire with your nasty little calendar. I'd like to light the fire with your nasty little boy!'

With a final snort of fury he turned, still clasping Annabel in his arms, and staggered down the front steps. Weakly, stricken and (for the moment) speechless, they watched his departure from the top of the steps. He took to his heels as soon as he was in the road. But he was less fortunate than William. As he turned the corner and vanished from sight, already two policemen were in pursuit. He was screaming defiance at them as he ran.

'I'LL HAVE ONE MORE TRY,' SAID UNCLE FREDERICK, AND ENTERED THE ROOM. 'GOOD AFTERNOON,' HE BELLOWED.

Annabel's head wobbled over his shoulder and her bonnet dangled by a string.

Then, no longer speechless, they turned on William.

'I *told* you,' said Robert to them when there was a slight lull in the storm. 'You wouldn't take any advice. If it wasn't Christmas day I'd hang him myself.'

'But you won't let me *speak*!' said William plaintively. 'Jus' listen to me a minute. When I got to his house he

ANNABEL DID NOT MOVE.

said, he said mos' distinct, he said, "Please use this—"'

'William,' interrupted Mrs Brown with dignity. 'I don't know what's happened and I don't *want* to know but I shall tell your father *all* about it *directly* we get home.'

Uncle Frederick saw them off at the station the next day.

'Does your effort at truth continue today as well?' he said to William.

'I s'pose it's Boxing Day too,' said William. 'He din' mention Boxing Day. But I s'pose it counts with Christmas.'

'I won't ask you whether you've enjoyed yourself then,' said Uncle Frederick. He slipped another half-crown into William's hand. 'Buy yourself something with that. Your Aunt chose the Church History book and the instruments. I'm really grateful to you about— Well, I think Emma's right. I don't think she'll ever come again.'

187

The train steamed out. Uncle Frederick returned home. He had been too optimistic. Lady Atkinson was in the drawing-room talking to his wife.

'Of course,' she was saying, 'I'm not annoyed. I bear no grudge because I believe the boy's *possessed*! He ought to be ex – exercised . . . You know, what you do with evil spirits.'

It was the evening of William's return home. His father's question as to whether William had been good had been answered as usual in the negative and, refusing to listen to details of accusation or defence (ignoring William's, 'But he *said* mos' distinct, he said, "Please use this—"' and the rest of the explanation always drowned by the others), he docked William of a month's pocket money. But William was not depressed. The ordeal of Christmas was over. Normal life stretched before him once more. His spirits rose. He wandered out into the lane. There he met Ginger, his bosom pal, with whom on normal days he fought and wrestled and carried out deeds of daring and wickedness, but who (like William) on festivals and holy days was forced reluctantly to shed the light of his presence upon his own family. From Ginger's face, too, a certain gloom cleared as he saw William.

'Well,' said William, ''v you enjoyed it?'

'I had a pair of braces from my aunt,' said Ginger bitterly. 'A pair of *braces*!'

'Well, I had a tie an' a Church History book.'

'I put my braces down the well.'

'I chopped up my tie into little bits.'

'Was it nice at your aunt's?'

William's grievances burst out.

'I went to church an' took what that man said an' I've been speaking the truth one with another an' leadin' a higher life an' well, it jolly well din't make it the happiest Christmas of my life what he said it would . . . It made it the worst. Every one mad at me all the time. I think I was the only person in the world speakin' the truth one with another an' they've took off my pocket money for it. An' you'd think 'f you was speakin' the truth yourself you might take what anyone else said for truth an' I keep tellin' 'em that he said mos' distinct, "Please use this house as if it were your own," but they won' listen to me! Well, I've done with it. I'm goin' back to deceit an' – an' – what's a word beginnin' with hyp—?'

'Hypnotism?' suggested Ginger after deep thought.

'Yes, that's it,' said William. 'Well, I'm goin' back to it first thing tomorrow mornin'.'

CHAPTER 9

AN AFTERNOON WITH WILLIAM

William's family was staying at the seaside for its summer holidays. This time was generally cordially detested by William. He hated being dragged from his well-known haunts, his woods and fields and friends and dog (for Jumble was not the kind of dog one takes away on a holiday). He hated the uncongenial atmosphere of hotels and boarding houses. He hated the dull promenades and the town gardens where walking over the grass and playing at Red Indians was discouraged. He failed utterly to understand the attraction that such places seemed to possess for his family. He took a pride and pleasure in the expression of gloom and boredom that he generally managed to maintain during the whole length of the holiday. But this time it was different. Ginger was staying with his family in the same hotel as William.

Ginger's father and William's father played golf together. Ginger's mother and William's mother looked at the shops and the sea together. William and Ginger went off together on secret expeditions. Though no cajoleries or coaxings would have persuaded William to admit that he was 'enjoying his holiday', still the presence of Ginger made it difficult for him to maintain his usual aspect of gloomy scorn. They hunted for smugglers in the caves, they slipped over seaweedy rocks and fell into the pools left by the retreating tide. They carried on warfare from trenches which they made in the sand, dug mines and counter-mines and generally got damp sand so deeply ingrained in their clothes and hair that, as Mrs Brown said almost tearfully, they 'simply defied brushing'.

Today they were engaged in the innocent pursuit of wandering along the front and sampling the various attractions which it offered. They stood through three performances of the Punch and Judy show, laughing uproariously each time. As they had taken possession of the best view and as it never seemed to occur to them to contribute towards the expenses, the showman finally ordered them off. They wandered off obligingly and bought two penny sticks of liquorice at the next stall. Then they bought two penny giant glasses of a biliousy-coloured green lemonade and quaffed them in front of the stall with intense enjoyment. Then they wandered away from the crowded part of the front to the empty space beyond the rocks. Ginger found a dead crab and William made a fire and tried to cook it, but the result was not encouraging.

191

They ate what was left of their liquorice sticks to take away the taste, then went on to the caves. They reviewed the possibility of hunting for smugglers without enthusiasm. William was feeling disillusioned with smugglers. He seemed to have spent the greater part of his life hunting for smugglers. They seemed to be an unpleasantly secretive set of people. They might have let him catch just one . . .

They flung stones into the retreating tide and leapt into the little pools to see how high they could make the splashes go.

Then they saw the boat . . .

It was lying by itself high and dry on the shore. It was a nice little boat with two oars inside.

'Wonder how long it would take to get to France in it?' said William.

'Jus' no time, I 'spect,' said Ginger. 'Why you can *see* France from my bedroom window. It must jus' be *no* distance – simply *no* distance.'

They looked at the boat in silence for a few minutes.

'It looks as if it would go quite easy,' said William.

'We'd have it back before whoever it is wanted it,' said Ginger.

'We couldn't do it any harm,' said William.

'It's simply *no* distance to France from my bedroom window,' said Ginger.

The longing in their frowning countenances changed to determination.

'Come on,' said William.

It was quite easy to push and pull the boat down to the water. Soon they were seated, their hearts triumphant and their clothes soaked with seawater, in the little boat and were being carried rapidly out to sea. At first William tried to ply the oars but a large wave swept them both away.

'Doesn't really matter,' said William cheerfully. 'The tide's takin' us across to France all right without botherin' with oars.'

For a time they lay back enjoying the motion and trailing fingers in the water.

''S almost as good as bein' pirates, isn't it?' said William.

At the end of half an hour Ginger said with a dark frown:

'Seems to *me* we aren't goin' in the right d'rection for France. Seems to *me*, Cap'n, we've been swep' out of our course. I can't see no land anywhere.'

'Well, we mus' be goin' *somewhere*,' said William the optimist, 'an' wherever it is it'll be *int'resting*.'

'It *mightn't* be,' said Ginger, who was ceasing to enjoy the motion and was taking a gloomy view of life.

'Well, I'm gettin' jolly hungry,' said William.

'Well, I'm *not*' said Ginger.

William looked at him with interest.

'You're lookin' a bit pale,' he said with over-cheerful sympathy. 'P'raps it was the crab.'

Ginger made no answer.

'Or it might have been the liquorice *or* the lemonade,' said William with interest.

'I wish you'd shut up talking about them,' snapped Ginger.

'Well, I feel almost *dyin'* of hunger,' said William. 'In books they draw lots and then one kills the other an' eats him.'

'I wun't mind anyone killin' an' eatin' me,' said Ginger.

'I've nothin' to kill you with, anyway, so it's no good talkin' about it,' said William.

'Seems to me,' said Ginger raising his head from his gloomy contemplation of the waves, 'that we keep changin' the d'rection we're goin' in. We'll like as not end at America or China or somewhere.'

'An' our folks'll think we're drowned.'

'We'll prob'ly find gold mines in China or somewhere an' make our fortunes.'

'An' we'll come home changed an' old an' they won't know us.'

Their spirits rose.

Suddenly William called excitedly, 'I see land! Jus' *look*!'

They were certainly rapidly nearing land.

'Thank goodness,' murmured Ginger.

'An uninhabited island I 'spect,' said William.

'Or an island inhabited by wild savages,' said Ginger.

The boat was pushed gently on to land by the incoming tide.

Ginger and William disembarked.

'I don't care where we are,' said Ginger firmly, 'but I'm goin' to stop here all my life. I'm not goin' in that ole boat again.'

A faint colour had returned to his cheeks.

'You *can't* stop on an uninhabited island all your life,' said William aggressively. 'You'll *have* to go away. You needn't go an' eat dead crabs jus' before you start, but you can't live on an uninhabited island all your life.'

'Oh, do shut up talkin' about dead crabs,' said Ginger.

'Here's a hole in a hedge,' called William. 'Let's creep through and see what there is the other side. Creep, mind, an' don't breathe. It'll prob'ly be wild savages or cannibals or something.'

They crept through the hedge.

There in a wide green space some lightly clad beings

were dancing backwards and forwards. One in the front called out unintelligible commands in a shrill voice.

William and Ginger crept behind a tree.

'Savages!' said William in a hoarse whisper. 'Cannibals!'

'Crumbs!' said Ginger. 'What'll we do?'

The white-clad figures began to leap into the air.

'Charge 'em,' said William, his freckled face set in a determined frown. 'Charge 'em and put 'em to flight utterin' wild yells to scare 'em – before they've time to know we're here.'

'All right,' said Ginger, 'come on.'

'Ready?' said Willlam through set lips. 'Steady . . . Go!'

The New School of Greek Dancing was a few miles down the coast from where William and Ginger had originally set forth in the boat. The second afternoon open-air class was in progress. Weedy males and aesthetic-looking females dressed in abbreviated tunics with sandals on their feet and fillets round their hair, mostly wearing horn-rimmed spectacles, ran and sprang and leapt and gambolled and struck angular attitudes at the shrill command of the instructress and the somewhat unmusical efforts of the (very) amateur flute player.

'Now run . . . *so* . . . hands extended . . . *so* . . . left leg

196

up . . . *so* . . . head looking over shoulder . . . *so* . . . no, try
not to overbalance . . . that piece again . . . never mind the
music . . . just do as I say . . . *so* . . . *Ow* . . . *OW!*'

'*Go!*'

Two tornadoes rushed out from behind a tree and
charged wildly into the crowd of aesthetic and bony
revellers. With heads and arms and legs they fought and
charged and kicked and pushed and bit. They might have
been a dozen instead of two. A crowd of thin, lightly clad
females ran screaming indoors. One young man nimbly

WILLIAM AND GINGER RUSHED OUT FROM BEHIND
A TREE AND CHARGED WILDLY INTO THE CROWD
OF AESTHETIC AND BONY REVELLERS.

climbed a tree and another lay prone in a rose bush.

'We've put 'em to flight,' said William breathlessly, pausing for a moment from his labours.

'Yes,' said Ginger dispiritedly, 'an' what'll we do *next*?'

'Oh, jus' keep 'em at bay an' live on their food,' said William vaguely, 'an' p'raps they'll soon begin to worship us as gods.'

But William was unduly optimistic. The flute player had secured some rope from an outhouse and, accompanied by some other youths, he was already creeping up behind William. In a few moments' time William and Ginger found themselves bound to neighbouring trees. They struggled wildly. They looked a strange couple. The struggle had left them tieless and collarless. Their hair stood on end. Their faces were stained with liquorice juice.

'They'll eat us for supper,' said William to Ginger. 'Sure's Fate they'll eat us for supper. They're prob'ly boilin' the water to cook us in now. Go on, try'n *bite* through your rope.'

'I have tried,' said Ginger wearily. 'It's nearly pulled my teeth out.'

'I wish I'd told 'em to give Jumble to Henry,' said William sadly. 'They'll prob'ly keep him to themselves or sell him.'

'They'll be *sorry* they took my trumpet off me when

they hear I'm eaten by savages,' said Ginger with a certain satisfaction.

The Greek dancers were drawing near by degrees from their hiding places.

'*Mad!*' they were saying. 'One of them *bit* me and he's probably got hydrophobia. I'm going to call on my doctor.' 'He simply *charged* me in the stomach. I think it's given me appendicitis.' '*Kicked* my leg. I can *see* the bruise.' '*Quite* spoilt the atmosphere.'

'William,' said Ginger faintly, 'isn't it funny they talk English? Wun't you expect them to talk some savage language?'

'I speck they've learnt it off folks they've eaten.'

From the open window of the house behind the trees came the loud tones of a lady who was evidently engaged in speaking through a telephone.

'Yes, *wild* . . . absolutely *mad* . . . *must* have escaped from the asylum . . . no one escaped from the asylum? . . . then they must have been *going* to the asylum and escaped on the *way* . . . well, if they aren't *lunatics* they're *criminals*. Please send a large *force*.'

It was when two stalwart and quite obviously English policemen appeared that William's bewilderment finally took from him the power of speech.

'Crumbs!' was all he said.

He was quite silent all the way home. He coldly repulsed all the policemen's friendly overtures.

Mrs Brown screamed when from the lounge window she saw her son and his friend approaching with their escort. It was Mr Brown who went boldly out to meet them, paid vast sums of hush money to the police force and brought in his son by the scruff of his neck.

MR BROWN PAID VAST SUMS OF HUSH MONEY TO THE POLICE FORCE AND BROUGHT IN HIS SON BY THE SCRUFF OF THE NECK.

'Well,' said William almost tearfully, at the end of a long and painful course of home truths, "f they'd reely *been* cannibals and eaten me you'd p'raps have been *sorry.*'

Mr Brown, whose peace had been disturbed and reputation publicly laid low by William's escort and appearance, looked at him.

'You flatter yourself, my son,' he said with bitterness.

'What'll we do today?' said Ginger the next morning.

'Let's start with watchin' the Punch and Judy,' said William.

'I'm not goin' in no boats,' said Ginger firmly.

'All right,' said William cheerfully, 'but if we find another dead crab I've thought of a better way of cooking it.'

CHAPTER 10

WILLIAM SPOILS THE PARTY

The Botts were going to give a fancy dress dance at the Hall on New Year's Eve, and William and all his family had been invited. The inviting of William, of course, was the initial mistake, and if only the Botts had had the ordinary horse sense (it was Robert who said this) not to invite William the thing might have been a success. It wasn't as if they didn't know William. If they hadn't known William, Robert said, one might have been sorry for them, but knowing William and deliberately inviting him to a fancy dress dance – well, they jolly well deserved all they got.

On the other hand William's own family didn't . . . and it was jolly hard lines on them (again I quote Robert) . . . Knowing that they had William all day and every day at home, anyone would think they'd have had the decency to invite them out without him . . . I mean whatever you said or whatever you did, you couldn't prevent it . . . he spoilt your life wherever he went.

But the Botts (of Botts' Famous Digestive Sauce) had a

ballroom that held 200 guests and they wanted to fill it. Moreover the Botts had a cherished daughter of tender years named Violet Elizabeth, and Violet Elizabeth, with her most engaging lisp and that hint of tears that was her most potent weapon, had said that she wanted her friendth to be invited too an' she'd thcream an' thcream an' *thcream* till she was *thick* if they din't invite her friendth to the party too . . .

'All right, pet,' had said Mr Bott soothingly. 'After all we may as well give a real slap-up show while we're about it and swell out the whole place – kids an' all.'

Mr Bott was 'self-made' and considering all things had made quite a decent job of himself, but his manners had not the 'repose that stamps the caste of Vere de Vere'. Violet Elizabeth on the other hand had been brought up from infancy in the lap of luxury and refinement provided by the successful advertising of Botts' Famous Digestive Sauce.

The delight with which Robert and Ethel (William's elder brother and sister) received the invitation to the fancy dress dance was, as I have said, considerably tempered by the fact of William's inclusion in the invitation. And William, with his natural perversity, was eager to go.

'Any show we *want* him to go to,' said Robert bitterly,

'he raises Cain about, but when a thing like this comes along – a thing that he'll completely spoil for us if he comes like he always does—' he spread out his arm with the eloquent gesture of one tried almost beyond endurance, and left the sentence unfinished.

'Well, let's accept for ourselves, and say that William can't go because he's got a previous engagement,' suggested Ethel.

'But I haven't,' said William indignantly. 'I haven't got anything at all wrong with me. I'm quite well. An' I *want* to go. I don' see why everyone else should go but me. Besides,' using an argument that he knew would appeal to them, 'you'll all be there an' you'll be able to see I'm not doing anything wrong, but if I was alone at home you wouldn't know what I was doing. Not,' he added hastily, 'that I *want* to do anything wrong. All I want to do is to make others happy. An' I'll have a better chance of doin' that at a party than if I was all alone at home.'

These virtuous sentiments did but increase the suspicious distrust of his family. The general feeling was that far worse things happened when William was out to be good than when he was frankly out to be bad.

'Oh, I think William must go,' said Mrs Brown in her placid voice. 'It will be so interesting for him and I'm sure he'll be good.'

Mrs Brown's rather pathetic faith in William's latent powers of goodness was unshared by any other of his family.

'Anyway,' she went on hastily, seeing only incredulity on the faces around her, 'the thing to do now is to decide what we're all going as.'

'I think I'll go as a lion,' said William. 'I should think you could buy a lionskin quite cheap.'

'Oh, *quite*!' said Robert sarcastically. 'Why not shoot one while you're about it?'

'Yes, an' I will,' said William, ''f you'll show me one. I bet my bow and arrow could kill a few lions.'

'No William, darling,' interposed Mrs Brown again quickly, 'I think you'd find a lionskin too hot for a crowded room.'

'But I wun't go into the room,' said William, 'I want to crawl about the garden in it roarin' an' springin' out at folks – scarin' 'em.'

'And you just said you wanted to go to make people *happy*,' said Robert sternly.

'Well, that'd make 'em happy,' said William unabashed. 'It'd be *fun* for 'em.'

'*Not* a lion, darling,' said his mother firmly.

'Well a brigand then,' suggested William, 'a brigand with knives all over me.'

Mrs Brown shuddered.

'*No*, William . . . I believe Aunt Emma has a fancy dress suit of Little Lord Fauntleroy that Cousin Jimmie once wore. I expect she'd lend it, but I'm not sure whether it wouldn't be too small.'

Wild shouts greeted this suggestion.

'Well,' William said offended, 'I don' know who he was but I don' know why you should think of me bein' him so funny.'

The Little Lord Fauntleroy suit proved too small, much to the relief of William's family, but another cousin was found to have a Page's costume which just fitted William. It certainly did not suit him. As Mrs Brown put it, 'I don't know quite what's wrong with the costume but somehow it looks so much more attractive off than on.'

Robert was to go as Henry V and Ethel as Night.

William, to his delight, found that all the members of his immediate circle of friends (known to themselves as the Outlaws) had been invited to the fancy dress dance. All had wished to go as animals or brigands or pirates, but family opposition and the offer of the loan of costumes from other branches of their families had been too strong in every case. Ginger was to be an Ace of Clubs, Henry a Gondolier ('dunno what it is,' remarked Henry despondently, 'but you bet it's nothing exciting or they wouldn't have let me be it'). Douglas was to be a Goat Herd ('It's an ole Little Boy Blue set-out,' he explained mournfully, 'but I said I wouldn't go if they didn't call it something else. Not but what everyone'll *know*,' he ended gloomily).

'An' we could've been brigands s'easy, s'easy,' said Ginger indignantly. 'Why, you only want a shirt an' a pair of trousers an' a coloured handkerchief round your head an' a scarf thing round your waist with a few knives an' choppers an' things on it . . . No trouble at all for them, an' they jus' won't let us – jus' cause we want to.'

There was a short silence. Then William spoke. 'Well, *let's*,' he said. 'Let's get Brigands' things an' change into 'em when we've got there. They'll never know. They'll never notice. We'll hide 'em in the old summer house by the lake an' go an' change there, an' – an' we won't wear their rotten ole Boy Blues an' Gondowhatevritis. We'll be Brigands.'

'We'll be Brigands,' agreed the Outlaws joyfully.

The Botts were having a large house party for the occasion.

'Lord Merton is going to be there,' said Mrs Brown to her husband, looking up from her usual occupation of darning socks, as he entered the room. 'Just fancy! He's in the Cabinet! Mr Bott's got to know his son in business and he's coming down for it and going to stay the night.'

'*That* fellow!' snorted Mr Brown. 'He ought to be shot.' Mr Brown's political views were always very decided and very violent. 'He's ruining the country.'

'Is he dear?' said Mrs Brown in her usual placid voice. 'But I'm sure he'll look awfully nice as a Toreador. She says he's going as a Toreador.'

'Toreador!' snorted Mr Brown. 'Very appropriate too. He *is* a Toreador! – and we're the – bull. I tell you that man's policy is bringing the country to rack and ruin. When you're dying of starvation you can think of the fellow toreadoring – Toreador indeed! I wonder decent people have him in their houses. Toreador indeed! I tell you he's bleeding the country to death. He ought to be hung for murder. That man's policy, I tell you, is wicked – *criminal*. Leave him alone and in ten years' time he'll have wiped out half the population of England by slow starvation. He's killing trade. He's *ruining* the country.'

'Yes, dear,' murmured Mrs Brown, 'I'm sure you're right . . . I think these blue socks of yours are almost done, don't you?'

'*Ruining* it!' snorted Mr Brown, going out of the room and slamming the door.

William looked up from the table where he was engaged

theoretically in doing his homework. Practically he was engaged in sticking pins into the lid of his pencil case.

'Why's he not in prison if he's like that?' said William.

'Who, darling?' said Mrs Brown. 'Your father?'

'No, the man he was talking about. And what's a Toreador?'

'Oh . . . a man who fights bulls.'

William's spirits rose.

'Will there be bulls there?'

'I hope not, dear.'

'Shall I go as a bull? It seems silly to have a Tor— what you said, without a bull. I could easy get a bullskin. I 'spect the butcher'd give me one.'

Mrs Brown shuddered.

'No, dear, most certainly not. Now do get on with your homework.'

William, having fixed all his pins except one into the lid, now took the last pin and began to twang them with it. They made different noises according as they were twanged near the head or near the point. Mrs Brown looked up, then bent her head again over her darning . . . What funny things they taught children nowadays, she thought.

The day of the dance drew nearer. Robert was still feeling sore at the prospect of William's presence. He relieved his feelings by jeering at William's costume. William himself, as it happened, was not quite happy about the costume. It was a long stretch from the animal skin and Brigand's apparel of his fancy to this pale blue sateen of reality. When he heard a visitor, to whom Mrs Brown showed it, say that it was 'picturesque' his distrust of it grew deeper.

Robert was never tired of alluding to it. 'Won't William look sweet?' he would say, and 'Don't frown like that, William. That won't go with the little Prince Charming costume at all.'

William accepted these taunts with outward indifference, but no one insulted William with impunity. Robert might have taken warning from past experiences . . .

When not engaged in tempting the Fates by teasing William, Robert was engaged in trying to win the affection of a female epitome of all the virtues and graces who had come to stay with the Crewes for the dance. This celestial creature was called Glory Tompkins. Robert called her Gloire as being more romantic. At least he spelt it Gloire but pronounced it Glor. Through Robert's life there passed a never-ending procession of young females endowed with every beauty of form and soul. To each one in turn he sincerely vowed eternal fidelity. Each one was told in hoarse accents how from now onwards his whole life would be dedicated to making himself more worthy of her. Then after a week or two her startling perfection would seem less startling, and someone yet more perfect would dawn upon the horizon, shattering poor Robert's susceptible soul yet again. Fortunately the fidelity of these youthful radiant beings was about on a par with Robert's own . . . Anyway Glory was the latest, and Robert called on the Crewes every evening to tell Glory with his eyes (the expression that he fondly imagined to express lifelong passion as a matter of fact was suggestive chiefly of acute indigestion) or with his lips how empty and worthless his life had been till he met her . . .

William had his eye on the affair. He generally followed Robert's love affairs with interest, though it was difficult to keep pace with them. A handle against Robert was useful and more than once Robert's love affairs had afforded useful handles. Robert's physical size and strength made William wary in his choice of weapons, but it was generally William who scored . . .

On the day before the dance Robert had written a note to Miss Tompkins.

BELOVED GLOIRE (Robert preferred writing Gloire to saying it because he had a vague suspicion that he didn't pronounce it quite right),

You will know with what deep feelings I am looking forward to tomorrow. Will you have the 1st and 3rd and 4th and 7th and 8th with me. The 4th is the Blues you know that we have been practising. If it is fine and the moon is out shall we sit out the 1st in the rose garden on the seat by the sundial? It will be my first meeting with you for two days and I do not want it profaned by other people, who know, and care nothing of our deep feeling for each other, all about us. When the music starts will you be there? And just for the few sacred moments we will tell each other all that is in our souls. Then we will be gay for the rest of the evening, but the memory of those few sacred minutes of the first dance in the rose garden, just you and me and the moon and the roses, will be with us in our souls all the evening.

Your knight,
ROBERT.

He was going to take it himself though he knew that his idol had gone away for the day. However a friend hailed him just as he was setting out, so he put the note on the hatstand and went out to join his friend, meaning to take the note later.

He met William just coming in.

'Hello, little Page—' he said in mock affection.

William looked at him, his brows drawn into a frown, his most sphinx-like expression upon his freckled face. William's stubbly hair as usual stood up around his face like a halo . . . William was not beautiful.

Robert, whistling gaily, went down the steps to join his friend at the gate.

William took up the note, read the address, and went into the drawing-room where Mrs Brown was, as usual, darning socks.

'Sh' I take this note for Robert?' he said, assuming his earnestly virtuous expression. Mrs Brown was touched.

'Yes, dear,' she said, 'how thoughtful of you.'

An hour later Robert returned. 'I say,' he said, 'where's that note? I left a note here. Has it been taken round?'

'Yes, dear,' said Mrs Brown absently.

At that moment William was sitting on a gate far from the main road reading the note. On his face was a smile of pure bliss. There was a look of purpose in his eye.

The evening arrived. William as a Page, Ginger as Ace of Clubs, Douglas as a Goat Herd, Henry as a Gondolier, stood in a sheepish group and were gazed at proudly by their fond mothers. They looked far from happy, but the thought of the Brigands' clothes concealed in the summer house comforted them. Robert as Henry V was having a good deal of trouble with his costume. He had closed the vizor of his helmet and it refused to open. Several of his friends were trying to force it. Muffled groans came from within.

Violet Elizabeth was dressed as a Star. She was leaping up and down and squeaking, 'Look at me. I'm a thtar!' She shed stars at every leap, and an attendant nurse armed with needle and cotton sewed them on again.

Pierrots, peasant girls, harlequins, kings, queens, gypsies and representatives of every nationality filled the room. It was noticed, with no particular interest on anyone's part, that William the Page was no longer the centre of the sheepish group of fancy-dressed Outlaws. William the Page had crept into the ladies' dressing-room, and in the temporary absence of the attendant (who was engaged in carrying on an impromptu flirtation with a good-looking chauffeur in the drive) he purloined a lady's black velvet evening cloak and a filmy scarf. Fortunately the cloak had a hood . . .

Robert, helmetless and rather purple in the face as the result of his prolonged sojourn behind his vizor (from which he had finally been freed by a tin opener borrowed from the kitchen), came to the rose garden. Upon the seat that was the appointed trysting place a petite figure was awaiting him shrouded in a cloak.

'Glory!' breathed Robert softly.

The figure seemed to sway towards him, though its face was still completely hidden by its scarf and hood.

Robert slipped his strong arm round it, and it nestled on his shoulder.

'Just to think,' murmured Robert, 'that this time last week I didn't know you. You've given an entirely new meaning to my life – I feel that everything will be different now. I shall give up all my life to trying to be more worthy of you—'

The figure gave a sudden snort and Robert started.

'Glor! Are you ill?'

The figure hastily emitted a deep groan.

Robert sprang up.

'Glor,' he cried in distress. 'I'll get you some water. I'll call a doctor. I'll—'

He fled into the house, where he got a glass of water and actually found a doctor – a very unhappy doctor in a hired Italian costume that was too small for him. When he found the seat empty he turned upon Robert indignantly.

'But she *was* here,' said the bewildered Robert. 'I left her here in the most awful agony. My God, if she's dead.'

'If she's dead,' said the doctor coldly, 'I'm afraid I can't

'JUST TO THINK, DARLING,' MURMURED ROBERT, 'THAT
LAST WEEK I DIDN'T KNOW YOU. YOU'VE GIVEN A NEW
MEANING TO MY LIFE.'

do anything. I'm sorry to seem unsympathetic, but if you knew the pain it causes me to walk in these clothes you'd understand my saying that I'll let the whole world die in awful agony before I come out here again on your wild goose chase after dying females.'

Robert was hunting distractedly under all the bushes around the seat . . .

The Outlaws had changed their clothes. They stood arrayed as Brigands in all the glory of coloured scarves and handkerchiefs and murderous-looking weapons. Upon the floor lay the limp outer coating of the Page, the Ace of Clubs, the Gondolier and the Goat Herd. They leapt with joy and brandished kitchen choppers and bread knives and trowels.

'Now what're we going to *do*?' said Ginger.

'Everyone else is dancing,' suggested Douglas mildly.

'*Dancing!*' repeated William scornfully. 'D'you think we've put these things on to *dance*?'

'Well, what're we goin' to do?' said Ginger.

'There's one thing we mus' do first of all,' said William. He spoke in his leader's manner and his freckled face was stern. 'There's a man here dressed as a tor – as a bull killer.'

'A Toreador,' said Douglas with an air of superior knowledge.

217

William looked at him crushingly.

'Well – din' I say that?' he said, then turning to the others: 'Well, this man, this torrydoor man's been starvin' folks an' killin' 'em. I heard my father say so. Well, we've gotter *do* something – we may never get a chance of gettin' him again. He's a starver an' a murderer, I heard my father say so, an' we've gotter *do* something to him.'

'*How?*' said the Brigands.

'Well, you listen to me,' said William.

The Brigands gathered round.

William crept round the outside of the ballroom. Through the open window came the sound of the band, and, looking in, William could see couples of gaily dancing youths and maidens in fantastic dresses. Near one open window Henry V stood with a small and dainty Columbine.

'But it *is* my dance with you, Glor,' Henry V was saying hoarsely. 'I wrote to you and asked you, and oh, I'm so glad that you're better. I've been through hours of agony thinking you were dead.'

'You're absolutely mad,' Glory replied impatiently. 'I've no idea what you're talking about. You never wrote and you've never asked me for a dance. I've never seen you all evening till this minute, except in the distance with everyone trying to pull your head off. You shouldn't come

in a costume like that if you don't know how to open and
shut it, and now you suddenly come and begin to talk
nonsense about me being dead.'

'Glor—'

'I wish you'd *stop* calling me by that silly name.'

'But – Glor – Glory – you *must* have got my note. You
were in the rose garden. You let me put my arm round
you. I've been treasuring the memory all evening when
I wasn't racked with agony at the thought of you being
ill – or dead.'

'I *never* met you in the rose garden. You're *mad*!'

'I'm not. You did. Oh, Glor—'

'*Stop* calling me that. It sounds like a patent medicine
or a new kind of metal polish . . . and, as you don't care
for me enough to get a dance in decent time, and as you
go mooning about the garden with other girls – girls who
seem to go dying all over the place from your account –
and pretend you think they're me—'

'I didn't pretend. I thought it was. It must have been.
Oh, Glor—'

'*Stop* saying that! I've simply finished with you. Well, if
you don't care about me enough to know who *is* me and –
thank you, when I want to die I'll do it at home and not
in a beastly old rose garden – so *there* – And I've *finished*
with you, Robert Brown – so *there*.'

Columbine flounced off and Henry V, pale and distraught, pursued her with a ghostly, 'Oh, Glor—'

The Brigand passed on, a faint smile on his face.

The Toreador had found a quiet corner in the empty smoking-room and was relaxing his weary limbs in an armchair. He had indulged in a quiet smoke and was now indulging in a quiet doze . . . He did not like dancing. He did not like wearing fancy dress. He did not like the Botts. He did not like the noise of the band. He did not like anything . . .

He opened his eyes with a start, conscious of an alien presence. By his side he saw a small and very villainous-looking Brigand with a stern freckled face, a row of gardening tools and a carving knife round his waist and a red handkerchief tied round his head.

'There's a Russian wants to see you,' said the Brigand in a dramatic whisper. 'He's waiting for you in the coach-house. He's gotter message for you from the Russians – private.'

The Toreador sat up and rubbed his eyes. The Brigand was still there.

'Please say it again,' said the Toreador.

'There's a Russian wants to see you. He's waiting for you in the coach-house. He's gotter message for you from the Russians,' repeated the Brigand.

220

'Where did you say he was?' said the Toreador.

'In the coach-house.'

'And what do you say he's got?'

'A message from the Russians.'

'What Russians?'

'All the Russians.'

'Good Lord!' said the Toreador. 'Just pinch me, will you?'

William obeyed without a flicker of expression upon his face.

'Still here,' said the Toreador in a resigned tone of voice. 'I thought it might be a nightmare. Well, there's no harm in going to see. What's he like?'

'Oh – just like a Russian,' said William vaguely. 'Russian clothes an' Russian face an' – an' – Russian boots.'

'How did he get here?'

'Walked,' said William calmly. 'Walked all the way from Russia.'

'Does he speak English?'

'No. Russian.'

'How do you know what he says then?'

'I learn Russian at school,' said William with admirable presence of mind.

'You're a linguist,' commented the Toreador.

'No, I'm not,' corrected William. 'I'm English like you.'

They were on the way to the coach-house.

'I may as well see it through,' said the Toreador. 'It's so intriguing. It's like *Alice in Wonderland*. A Russian brought a message from all the Russians and walked all the way from Russia. He must have started when he was quite a child. It's better than being bored to death watching idiots making still greater idiots of themselves.'

'This is the coach-house,' said the Brigand.

'It's dark.'

'Yes,' said the Brigand. 'He's right in the corner over there. He's just having a little sleep.'

The Toreador stepped into the coach-house. The door was immediately slammed and bolted from outside. The Toreador took out his pocket torch and looked round the room. It was empty. No Russian in Russian boots, etc., with a message from all the Russians, slept in a corner. The only means of exit were the door and a barred window. He went to the barred window. Four small stern Brigands stood outside.

'I say,' said the Toreador. 'Look here—'

The freckled frowning Brigand who had led him there spoke.

'We're not going to let you out,' he said, 'till you've promised to go away from England and never come back.'

'But *why*?' said the Toreador. 'Why should I? I know it's all a dream. But just tell me why I should, anyway.'

'Because you're starvin' an' killin' folks,' said the Brigand sternly. 'You're ruinin' the country.'

'I do hope I remember all this when I wake up,' said the Toreador. 'It's too priceless. But look here, if you don't let me out I'll kick the door down. I've never starved anyone and I've never killed anyone, and I—'

'We don' want to argue,' said William remembering a frequent remark of his father's and trying to imitate his tone of voice, 'but we're not goin' to let you out till you promise to go out of England and never come back.'

With that the Brigands turned and went slowly back to the house. The sound of a mighty kick against the coach-house door followed them into the night.

'What we goin' to do *now*?' said Ginger.

'Oh, jus' look round a bit,' said William.

Again they went round the outside of the house passing by each open window. Just inside one sat Henry V with a very demure Spring.

'I can't tell you what a difference it's made to me getting to know you—' Henry V was saying.

By another a group of people stood around a – yes – the Brigands rubbed their eyes, but there he was – a Toreador.

A tall angular Helen of Troy, well past her first youth

223

'I SAY,' SAID THE TOREADOR, 'IF YOU DON'T LET ME OUT
I'LL KICK THE DOOR DOWN.'

'WE'RE NOT GOING TO LET YOU OUT,' SAID WILLIAM,
'TILL YOU PROMISE TO GO OUT OF ENGLAND, AND
NEVER COME BACK.'

and quite obviously never having possessed a face that
could launch a thousand ships, was sitting in the window
recess with an emaciated Henry VIII. 'Look,' she was
saying, 'that Toreador's Lord Merton – on the Cabinet,
you know, quite important.'

225

The Brigands gaped at each other.

A few minutes later Helen of Troy, looking down, saw a small meek boy dressed in a sort of pirate's costume sitting by her.

'Please,' he said politely, 'would you kin'ly tell me who that man in a bull fighter's dress is.'

'That's Lord Merton, dear,' said Helen of Troy kindly. 'He's in the Cabinet. Do you know what that means?'

'Then is there – are there two Toreadors?'

'Yes. The other's Mr Jocelyn. He's a writer, I believe. Nobody important.'

'We've took the wrong one,' said William in a hoarse whisper, as he rejoined the Brigands. 'There was two.'

'Crumbs!' said the Brigands aghast.

'What we goin' to do *now*?' said Ginger.

William was not one to relinquish a task half done. 'We'll have to put this one in an' let the other out,' he said.

A few minutes later the Toreador came out on to the lawn smoking a cigar.

'If you please,' said a miniature Brigand, who seemed to rise up from the ground at his feet, 'someone wants to see you special. He says he's a German with a message quite private. He doesn't want anyone else to know.'

'Ha!' snorted the Toreador throwing away his cigar. 'Show me, boy.'

He followed William to the coach-house. The other Brigands came behind a-thrill for whatever would happen. William flung open the door of the coach-house. The second Toreador entered. The first Toreador, who had by this time completely lost sight of any humorous aspect the affair might previously have had in his eyes, and had worked himself up into a blind fury, sprang upon the second Toreador as he entered and threw him to the ground. The second Toreador pulled the first down with him, and they fought fiercely in the dark upon the floor of the coach-house, with inarticulate bellows of rage and rendings of clothes and hurling of curses . . .

Aghast, and apprehensive of consequences, the Brigands turned and went quickly towards the house so as to be as far as possible from the scene of the crime.

But all was changed at the house. There was no dancing. The band was mute. In the middle of the ballroom was a little heap of clothes, a Page's costume, an Ace of Club's costume, a Gondolier's costume, and a Goat Herd's costume, and over it stood four distraught mothers. Mrs Brown was almost hysterical. The guests stood in wondering groups around.

'The clothes have been found near the lake,' sobbed Mrs Brown.

'There's no trace of them anywhere,' sobbed Ginger's mother.

'The grounds have been searched.'

'They're nowhere in the house.'

'They must have taken off their clothes to swim.'

'And they're *drowned*.'

'*Drowned*.'

'Now don't take on,' said Mrs Bott soothingly to the distraught mothers, 'don't take on so, dearies. Botty'll have the lake dragged at once. There's nothing to worry about.'

The mothers went down to the lake followed by the whole assembly. The Brigands, feeling that the situation had got far beyond their control, followed cautiously in the rear keeping well in the shadow of the bushes.

It was bright moonlight. All the guests stood round the lake gazing with mournful anticipation at its calm surface. The mothers clung to each other sobbing.

'He was always such a *good* boy,' sobbed Mrs Brown. 'And he looked so *sweet* in his little blue suit.'

Henry V, with one arm round Spring, was leaning over the lake and vaguely fishing in it with a garden rake that he had picked up near by. 'You didn't know him, of course,' he said to Spring, 'but he was such a dear little chap and so fond of me.'

Then the Toreadors arrived, torn and battered and cobwebby and grimy. 'Where are they?' they panted as they ran. 'We've been insulted. We've been outraged. We've been *shamefully* treated. We demand those boys. We – *ah*!'

They caught sight of four Brigands cowering behind the bushes, and sprang at them.

The Brigands fled from them towards the lake. Henry V and Spring blocked William's way. He pushed them to one side, and both fell with a splash into the lake.

Then the guests and Fate closed round the Brigands.

In the scene of retribution that followed Robert showed himself unsympathetic, even glorying in William's afflictions . . . For a whole week after the fancy dress dance Robert repeatedly proclaimed that William had spoilt his life again.

'She'll never look at me now, of course,' he said bitterly to his mother. 'How could she look at the brother of the boy who nearly drowned her? And the only girl I've ever met who really understood me. And her mother says she's had a cold in her head ever since.'

'What was her name? Glory something, wasn't it, dear?'

'No, Mother,' impatiently. 'That's a girl I knew *ever* so long ago, and who never really understood me. This one—' William entered and Robert stopped abruptly.

'How do you like those new socks I made for you, dear?' said his mother to William. 'Are they all right?'

William felt that his hour had come. He'd had a rotten time but he was going to do just a little scoring on his own.

'Yes,' said William slowly, 'and just to think that this time last week I didn't know them. They've given an entirely new meaning to my life. I shall give up all my life trying to be more worthy of them. I've not got them on now because I don't want them profaned by people who don' know or care about them—' Then William gave a little groan and flopped into a chair in a fainting position.

'*William*,' said Mrs Brown, 'what *ever's* the matter with you?'

But Robert had gone a deep purple and was creeping quickly from the room.

William watched him, smoothing back his unsmoothable hair.

'Oh, Glor!' he ejaculated softly.

CHAPTER 11

THE CAT AND THE MOUSE

William's signal failure as a student of science was not due to any lack of interest. It was due to excess of zeal rather than to lack of zeal. William liked to experiment. He liked to experiment with his experiments. He liked to put in one or two extra things and see what happened. He liked to heat things when he was not told to heat them just to see what happened. And strange things happened. On several occasions William was deprived of his eyebrows and front hair. William in this condition felt proud of himself. He felt that everyone who saw him must imagine him to be the hero of some desperate adventure. He cultivated a stern frown with his hairless eyebrows. Old Stinks the Science Master rather liked William. He kept him in for hours in the lab after school washing up innumerable test tubes and cleaning the benches as atonement for his unauthorised experiments; but he would generally stay there himself, as well, smoking by the fire and drawing from William his views on life in general. On more than one occasion he gravely accepted from William the peace offering of a liquorice stick. In spite of William's really well-meant efforts, Old Stinks generally had to rewash all the test tubes and other implements when William had gone. Occasionally he invited William to tea and sat fascinated at the sight of the vast amount of nourishment that William's frame seemed able to assimilate. In return William lent him his original stories and plays to read (for William rather fancied himself as an author and had burnt much midnight candle over 'The Hand of Deth' and 'The Tru Story of an Indian Brave'). It is not too much to say that 'Stinks' enjoyed these far more than he did many works of better known authors.

But this term Old Stinks, having foolishly contracted Scarlet Fever on the last day of the holidays, was absent and his place was taken by Mr Evelyn Courtnay, an elegant young man with spats, very sleek hair and a microscopic moustache. From the moment he first saw him William felt that Mr Evelyn Courtnay was the sort of man who would dislike him intensely. His fears were not ill-founded. Mr Courtnay disliked William's voice and William's clothes and William's appearance. He disliked everything about William. It is only fair to add that this dislike was heartily reciprocated by William. William, however, was quite willing to lie low. It was Mr Courtnay who opened the campaign. He set William a hundred lines for

overbalancing on his stool in an attempt to regain a piece of
his litmus paper that had been taken with felonious intent
by his vis-à-vis. When William expostulated he increased
it to three hundred. When William, turning back to his
desk and encountering a whiff of hydrochloric acid gas
of his neighbour's manufacture, sneezed, he increased it
to four hundred. Then came a strange time for William.
William had previously escaped scot-free for most of his
crimes. Now to his amazement and indignation he found
himself in the unfamiliar position of a scapegoat. Any
disturbance in William's part of the room was visited
on William and quite occasionally William was not
guilty of it. Mr Evelyn Courtnay, having taken a dislike
to William, gratified his dislike to the full. Most people
considered that this was very good for William, but it was
a view that was not shared by William himself. He wrote
lines in most of his spare time and made a thorough and
systematic study of Mr Courtnay. Silently he studied his
habits and his mode of life and his character. He did this
because he had a vague idea that Fate might some day
deliver his enemy into his hand.

William rarely trusted Fate in vain . . . He gleaned
much of his knowledge of the ways of Mr Courtnay from
Eliza, Mr Courtnay's maid, who occasionally spent the
evening with Ellen, the Browns' housemaid.

''Is aunt's comin' to dine wif 'im tomorrer night,' said Eliza one evening.

William, who was whittling sticks in the back garden near the open kitchen door, put his penknife in his pocket, scowled and began to listen.

'Yes, it's goin' to be a set out an' no mistake,' went on Eliza. 'From what I makes out 'e's expectin' of money from 'er an' – oh my! the fuss – such a set out of a dinner an' all! I can't abide a young man what fusses to the hextent 'e does. An' 'e sez the larst time she 'ad dinner wif 'im she seed a mouse an' screamed the place down an' went orf in an 'uff so there's got to be mousetraps down in the dining-room all night before she comes as well as all the hother fuss.'

'Well, I never!' said Ellen.

William took out his penknife and moved away in search of fresh sticks to whittle.

But he moved away thoughtfully.

The next morning William had a science lesson. He was still thoughtful. Mr Evelyn Courtnay was jocular and facetious. In the course of a few jocular remarks to the front row he said: 'The feline species is as abhorrent to me as it was to the great Napoleon. Contact with it destroys my nerve entirely.'

234

'What's he mean?' whispered William to his neighbour.

'He means he don't like cats,' said William's neighbour.

'Well, why don't he say so then?' said William scornfully.

Someone near William dropped a test tube. Mr Courtnay turned his languid eye upon William.

'A hundred lines, Brown,' he said pleasantly.

'It wasn't me what did it, sir,' said William indignantly.

'Two hundred,' said Mr Courtnay.

'*Well!*' gasped William in outraged innocence.

'Four hundred,' said Mr Courtnay.

William was too infuriated to reply. He angrily mixed two liquids from the nearest bottles and heated them over his bunsen burner to relieve his feelings. There was a loud report. William blinked and wiped something warm off his face. His hand was bleeding from the broken glass.

Mr Courtnay watched from a distance.

'Six hundred,' he said as William took a bit of test tube from his hair, 'and to be done before Saturday, please.'

'Don't do 'em,' said Ginger as he walked homeward with William.

'Yes,' said William bitterly, 'an' that means go to the Head an' you know what *that* means.'

'Well, Douglas 'n Henry 'n me'll all help,' said Ginger.

William's countenance softened, then became sphinx-like.

'Thanks,' he said. 'I've thought of a better plan than that but thanks all the same.'

William walked slowly down the road. One hand was in his pocket. The other held a covered basket. He approached, with a stern frown and many cautious glances around him, the house of Mr Evelyn Courtnay. He entered the back gate warily. His entry did not suggest the welcome guest or even anyone who had the right of entry. There was something distinctly furtive about it. He made his way round to the house by the wall behind the bushes. He peeped in at the dining-room window. The perspiring Eliza was engaged in putting the last touches to the dining-table. He peeped into the drawing-room window. There sat Mr Evelyn Courtnay in the most elegant of elegant dress suits, engaged in the process of charming his aunt, Miss Felicia Courtnay. Miss Felicia Courtnay was elderly and grim and not very susceptible to charm, but her nephew was doing his best. Through the open window William could hear plainly.

'Oh yes, I get on splendidly, Aunt. I'm so fond of children – devoted to them. In some ways, of course, teaching is a waste of my talents, but on the whole—'

It was here that William drew his hand from his pocket and noiselessly deposited something on the floor through the open window. The something scuttled along the floor by the skirting board. William withdrew into the shadow. Suddenly a piercing scream came from within.

'It's a *mouse*, Evelyn. Help! *Help! HELP!*'

More screams followed.

William peeped in at the window and enjoyed the diverting spectacle of Miss Felicia Courtnay standing on a chair holding up her skirts and screaming, and of Mr Evelyn Courtnay on his knees with the poker in one hand, trying to reach the mouse who had taken refuge beneath a very low sofa. It was at that moment that William took Terence from the basket and deposited him upon the floor. Now Terence, William's cat, though he disliked William intensely, was of a sociable disposition. He found himself in a strange room with a fire upon the hearth. He liked fires. He did not like the basket in which he had just made his journey with William. He did not wish to go in the basket again. He wished to stay in the room. He decided that the best policy was to make up to the occupants of the room in the hopes that they would allow him to sit on the hearthrug in front of the fire. He approached the only occupant he could see. Terence may have known that there was a mouse in the room or he may not. He was not interested. He was a lover of comfort only. He was no mouser.

Mr Evelyn Courtnay, who was now lying at full length on the floor trying to look beneath the low sofa, felt suddenly something soft and warm and furry and purring rub itself hard against his face. He sprang up with a yell and leapt upon the grand piano.

'The brute!' he screamed. 'The brute! It *touched* me.'

The episode seemed to have driven him into a state closely bordering on lunacy.

William's cat purred ingratiatingly at the foot of the grand piano.

'Catch the mouse!' screamed Miss Felicia Courtnay. 'Get down and catch the mouse!'

'CATCH THE MOUSE,' SCREAMED MISS FELICIA. 'GET DOWN AND CATCH THAT MOUSE.'

'I can't while that brute's in the room,' screamed Mr Evelyn Courtnay from the grand piano. 'I can't – I tell you. I can't bear 'em. It *touched* me!'

MR EVELYN COURTNAY SPRANG UP WITH A YELL AND
LEAPT UPON THE GRAND PIANO. 'THE BRUTE TOUCHED
ME!' HE SHOUTED.

'You *coward*! I'm going to faint in a minute.'

'So am I, I tell you. I can't get down. It's looking at me.'

'I shall never forget this – *never*! You *brute* – you –
you – *tyrant*—'

'I shan't either. Go away, you nasty beast, go *away*!'

At that moment two things happened. The mouse put its little whiskered head out of its retreat to reconnoitre and Terence, determined to make friends with this new and strange acquaintance, leapt upon the grand piano on to the very top of Mr Evelyn Courtnay. Two screams rent the air – one a fine soprano, one a fine tenor.

'I can see it. Oh, this will *kill* me!'

'Get *down*, you brute. Get *down*!'

At this critical moment William entered like a deus ex machina. He swooped down upon the mouse before it realised what was happening, caught it by its tail and dropped it through the open window. Then he picked up Terence and did the same with him. Miss Felicia Courtnay, tearful and trembling, descended from her chair and literally fell upon William's neck.

'Oh you *brave* boy!' she sobbed. 'You *brave* boy! What *should* I have done without you?'

'I happened to see you through the window trying to catch the mouse,' said William, looking at her with an inscrutable expression and wide innocent eyes, 'an' I di'n' want to disturb you by comin' in myself so I just put the cat in an' when I saw that wasn't no good I jus' come in myself.'

Mr Evelyn Courtnay had descended hastily from his

grand piano and was smoothing his hair with both hands and glaring at William.

'Thank the dear little boy, Evelyn,' said Miss Felicia giving her nephew a cold glance. 'I don't know what I should have done without his protection. He practically saved my life.'

Mr Evelyn Courtnay glared still more ferociously at William and muttered threateningly.

'A little child rushing in where grown men fear to tread,' misquoted Miss Felicia sententiously, still beaming fondly at William. 'He must certainly stay to dinner after that.'

Mr Evelyn Courtnay, to his fury, had to provide William with a large meal to which William did full justice, munching in silence except when Miss Felicia's remarks demanded an answer. Miss Felicia ignored her nephew and talked with fond and grateful affection to William only. It was William who volunteered the information that her nephew taught him science.

'I hope he's kind to you,' said Miss Felicia.

William gave her a pathetic glance like one who wishes to avoid a dark and painful subject.

'I – I expect he means to be,' he said sadly.

William departed immediately after dinner. He seldom risked an anticlimax. He possessed the artistic instinct. Mr Evelyn Courtnay accompanied him to the door.

'No need to talk of this, my boy,' said Mr Courtnay with elaborate nonchalance.

William made no answer.

'And no need to do those lines,' said Mr Courtnay.

'Thank you,' said William. 'Good night.'

He walked briskly down the road. He'd enjoyed the evening. Its only drawback was that he could never tell anyone about it. For William, with all his faults, was a sportsman.

But he'd scored! He'd scored! He'd scored!

And Old Stinks was coming back next week!

Unable to restrain his feelings, William turned head over heels in the road.

CHAPTER 12

WILLIAM AND UNCLE GEORGE

It was William who bought the horn-rimmed spectacles. He bought them for sixpence from a boy who had bought them for a shilling from a boy to whose dead aunt's cousin's grandfather they had belonged.

William was intensely proud of them. He wore them in school all the morning. They made everything look vague and blurred, but he bore that inconvenience gladly for the sake of the prestige they lent him.

Ginger borrowed them for the afternoon and got all his sums wrong because he could not see the figures, but that was a trifling matter compared with the joy of wearing horn-rimmed spectacles. Douglas bagged them for the next day and Henry for the day after that. William had many humble requests for the loan of them from other boys which he coldly refused. The horn-rimmed spectacles were to be the badge of superiority of the Outlaws.

On the third day one of the masters who discovered that the horn-rimmed spectacles were the common property of William and his boon companions and were, optically

243

speaking, unnecessary, forbade their future appearance in school. The Outlaws then wore them in turn on the way to school and between lessons.

'My father,' said Douglas proudly, as he and William and Ginger strolled through the village together, ''s got a pair of spectacles an's gotter wear 'em *always*.'

'Not like these,' objected William who was wearing the horn-rimmed spectacles. 'Not great thick 'uns like these.'

'Well, anyway,' said Ginger. 'I've gotter aunt what's got false teeth.'

'That's nothin',' said William. 'False teeth isn't like spectacles. They look just like ornery teeth. You can't *see* they're false teeth.'

'No, but you can *hear* 'em,' said Ginger. 'They tick.'

'Well, anyway,' said Douglas, 'my cousin knows a man what's gotter false eye. It stays still while the other looks about.'

'Well,' said William determined not to be outdone, 'my father knows a man what's gotter false leg.'

'I think I remember once hearin',' said Ginger somewhat vaguely, ''bout a man with all false arms an' legs an' only his body real.'

'That's nothin',' said William giving rein to his glorious imagination. 'I once heard of a man with a false body an' only legs an' arms reel.'

His companions' united yell of derision intimated to him that he had overstepped the bounds of credulity, and, adjusting his horn-rimmed spectacles with a careless flourish, he continued unperturbed: 'Or I might have dreamed about him. I don' *quite* remember which.'

'I bet you *dreamed* about him,' said Ginger indignantly. 'I bet it isn't *possible*. How'd his stomach work 'f he hadn't gotter real one?'

'An' I bet it *is* possible,' said William stoutly. 'It'd work with machinery an' wheels an' springs an' things same as a clock works an' he'd hafter wind it up every mornin'.'

The other Outlaws were impressed by William's tone of certainty.

'Well,' said Ginger guardedly, 'I don' say it isn't *possible*. I only say it isn't *prob'le*.'

The vast knowledge of the resources of the English language displayed by this remark vaguely depressed the others, and they dropped the subject hastily.

'I can walk like a man with a false leg,' said William, and he began to walk along, swinging one stiff leg with a flourish.

'Well, I can click my teeth 's if they was false,' said Ginger, and proceeded to bite the air vigorously.

'I bet I can look 's if I had a glass eye,' said Douglas,

making valiant if unsuccessful efforts to keep one eye still and roll the other.

They walked on in silence, each of them wholly and frowningly absorbed in his task, William limping stiffly, Ginger clicking valiantly, and Douglas rolling his eyes.

A little short-sighted man who met them stopped still and stared in amazement.

'Dear me!' he said.

'I've gotter false leg,' William condescended to explain, 'and *he*,' indicating Douglas, ''s gotter glass eye, an' *he's* got false teeth.'

'Dear me!' gasped the little old man. 'How very extraordinary!'

They left him staring after them . . .

Douglas, wildly cross-eyed, set off at the turning to his home. He was labouring under the delusion that he had at last acquired the knack of keeping one eye still while he rolled the other, though William and Ginger informed him repeatedly that he was mistaken.

'They're *both* movin'.'

'They're *not*, I tell you. One's keepin' still. I can feel it keepin' still.'

'Well, we can *see* it, can't we? We oughter know.'

'I don' care what you can *see*. I know what I *do*, don' I?

It's *my* eye an' I move it an' *I* oughter be able to tell when I'm *not* movin' it . . . So *there*!'

He rolled both eyes at them fiercely as he departed.

William and Ginger went on together, stumping and clicking with great determination. Suddenly they both stopped.

On the footpath just outside a door that opened straight on to the street, stood a bath-chair. In it were a rug and a scarf.

'Here's my bath-chair,' said William. ''S tirin' walkin' like this with a false leg all the time.'

He sat down in the chair with such a jerk that his horn-rimmed spectacles fell off. Though it was somewhat of a relief to see the world clearly, he missed the air of distinction that he imagined they imparted to him and, picking them up, adjusted them carefully on his nose. The sensation of being the possessor of both horn-rimmed spectacles and a false leg had been a proud and happy one. He wrapped the rug around his knees.

'You'd better push me a bit,' he said to Ginger. ''S not tirin' havin' false teeth. You oughter be the one to push.'

But Ginger, unlike William, was not quite lost in his role.

'It's not our bath-chair. Someone'll be comin' out an' makin' a fuss if we start playin' with it. Besides,' with

247

some indignation, 'how d'you know havin' false teeth isn't tirin'? Ever tried 'em? An' let me *tell* you clickin' *is* tirin'. It's makin' my jaws ache somethin' terrible.'

'Oh, come on!' said William impatiently. 'Do stop talkin' about your false teeth. Anyway it couldn't rest your *jaws* ridin' in a *chair*, could it? A *chair* couldn't rest your jaw *or* your teeth, could it? Well, it *could* rest my false leg an', anyway, we'll only go a bit an' whoever it is won't miss it before we bring it back, an' anyway I don't suppose they mind lendin' it to help a pore ole man with a false leg an' another with false teeth.'

'Not much helpin' *me* pushin' *you*!' said Ginger bitterly.

'Your false teeth seems to be makin' you very grumpy!' said William severely. 'Oh, come on! They'll be comin' out soon.'

Ginger began to push the bath-chair at first reluctantly, but finally warmed to his task. He tore along at a breakneck speed. William's face was wreathed in blissful smiles. He held the precious horn-rimmed spectacles in place with one hand and with the other clutched on to the side of the bath-chair, which swayed wildly as Ginger pursued his lightning and uneven way. They stopped for breath at the end of the street.

'You're a jolly good pusher!' said William.

Praise from William was rare. Ginger, in spite of his breathlessness, looked pleased.

'Oh, that's nothin',' he said modestly. 'I could do it ten times as fast as that. I'm a bit tired of false teeth though. I'm goin' to stop clickin' for a bit.'

William tucked in his rug and adjusted his spectacles again.

'Do I look like a pore old man?' he said proudly.

Ginger gave a scornful laugh.

'No, you don't. You've gotter boy's face. You've got no lines nor whiskers nor screwedupness like an old man.'

William drew his mouth down and screwed up his eyes into a hideous contortion.

'Do I now?' he said as clearly as he could through his distorted mask of twisted muscles.

Ginger looked at him dispassionately.

'You look like a kinder monkey now,' he said.

William took the long knitted scarf that was at the bottom of the bath-chair and wound it round and round his head and face till only his horn-rimmed spectacles could be seen.

'Do I now?' he said in a muffled voice.

Ginger stared at him in critical silence for a minute and said, 'Yes, you do now. At least you look's if you might be *anything* now.'

'All right,' said William in his far-away muffled voice. 'Pretend I'm an old man. Wheel me back no . . . *slowly*, mind 'cause I'm an old man!'

They began the return journey. Ginger walked very slowly, chiefly because it was uphill and he was still out of breath. William leant back feebly in his chair enjoying the role of aged invalid, his horn-rimmed spectacles peering out with an air of deep wisdom from a waste of woollen muffler.

Suddenly a woman who was passing stopped.

'Uncle George!' she said in a tone of welcome and surprise.

She was tall and thin and grey-haired and skittish-looking and gaily dressed.

'Well, this *is* a pleasant surprise,' she said. 'When you didn't answer our letter we thought you really weren't going to come to see us. We really did. And now I find you on your way to our house. *What* a treat for us! I'd have known you anywhere, *dear* Uncle George, even if I hadn't recognised the bath-chair and the muffler that I knitted for you on your last birthday. How *sweet* of you to wear it! And you're looking *so* well!' She dropped a vague kiss upon the woollen muffler and then turned to Ginger. 'This little boy can go. I can take you on to the house.' She slipped a coin into Ginger's hand. 'Now run away little boy! I'll look after him.'

Ginger, after one bewildered look, fled, and the lady began to push William's chair along briskly. William was so entirely taken aback that he could for the moment devise no plan of action, and meekly allowed himself to be propelled down the village street. With an instinctive desire to conceal his identity he had pulled the rug up to his elbows and arranged the flowing ends of the all-enveloping scarf to cover the front of his coat. Wistfully he watched Ginger's figure which was fast disappearing in the distance. Then the tall female bent down and shouted into his ear.

'And how *are* you, dear Uncle George?'

William looked desperately round for some chance of escape, but saw none. Feeling that some reply was necessary, and not wishing to let his voice betray him he growled.

'So glad,' yelled the tall lady into the muffler. 'So glad. If you *think* you're better, you *will* be better you know, as I always used to tell you.'

To his horror, William saw that he was being taken in through a large gateway and up a drive. He felt as though he had been captured by some terrible enemy. Would he ever escape? What would the dreadful woman do to him when she found out? He couldn't breathe, and he could hardly see, and he didn't know what was going to happen to him . . . He growled again rather ferociously, and she leant down to the presumptive region of his ear and shouted.

'*Much* better, dear Uncle George! . . . *Ever* so much better . . . it's only a question of *will*power.'

She left him on a small lawn and went through an opening in the box hedge. William could hear her talking to some people on the other side.

'He's *come*! Uncle George's *come*!' she said in a penetrating whisper.

'Oh, *dear*!' said another voice. 'He's *so* trying! What shall we do?'

'He's *wealthy*. Anyway we may as well try to placate him a bit.'

'Hush! He'll hear you.'

'Oh, no, he's been as deaf as a post for years.'

'How did you meet him, Frederica, darling?'

'I met him *quite* by accident,' said Frederica darling in her shrill and cheerful voice. 'He was being brought here by a boy.'

'And did you recognise him? It's ten years since you saw him last.'

'I recognised the bath-chair. It's the one poor, dear Aunt Ferdinanda used to have, and the darling was wearing that scarf I knitted for him. Oh, but I think I'd have recognised the old man anyway. He hasn't changed a bit; though he's dreadfully muffled up. You know he was always so frightened of fresh air . . . and he's shrunk a bit, I think . . . you know, old people do – and I'm afraid he's as touchy as ever. He was *quite* huffy on the way here because I said that if he'd *will* to be well he *would* be well. That always annoyed him, but I must be true to my principles, mustn't I?'

'Hadn't someone better go to him? Won't it annoy him to be left alone?'

'Oh, I don't know. He's not sociable, you know – and as deaf as a post and—'

'Perhaps you'd better explain to the boys, Frederica—'

'Oh *yes*! It's your Great-Uncle George, you know – *ever* so old, and we've not seen him for *ten* years, and he's just come to live here with his *male* attendant, you know – taken a furnished house, and though we asked him to come to see us (he's most *eccentric*, you know – simply won't see *anyone* at his own house) he never even answered and we thought he must still be annoyed. I told him the last time I saw him, ten years ago, that if only he'd think he could walk, he'd be *able* to walk, and it annoyed him, but I must be true to my principles – anyway to my surprise I found him on his *way* to our house this afternoon and—'

Frederica paused for breath.

'We'd better go to him, dear. He might be feeling lonely.'

William was far from lonely. He was listening with mingled interest and apprehension to the conversation on the other side of the hedge and revolving in his mind the question whether they'd see him if he crawled across the lawn to the gate – or perhaps it would be better to make a dash for it, tear off the rug and muffler and run for all he was worth to the gate and down the road.

He had almost decided to do that when they all suddenly appeared through the opening in the hedge. William gave a gasp as he saw them. First came Frederica, the tall and agile lady who had captured him, next a very old lady with a Roman nose and expression of grim determination and a pair of lorgnettes, next came a young curate, next a muscular young man in a college blazer, and last a little girl.

William knew the little girl.

Her name was Emmeline, and she went to the same school as William – and William detested her. William now allowed himself the slight satisfaction of putting out his tongue at her beneath his expanse of muffler.

But his heart sank as they surrounded him. They all

surveyed him with the greatest interest. He looked about desperately once more for some way of escape, but his opportunity had gone. Like the psalmist's enemies, they closed him in on every side. Nervously he pulled up his rug, spread out his muffler and crouched yet further down in his bath-chair.

'You remember Mother, dear Uncle George, don't you?' screamed Frederica into the muffler.

The dignified dame raised the lorgnettes and held out a majestic hand. William merely growled. He was beginning to find the growl effective. They all hastily took a step back.

'Sulking!' explained Frederica in her penetrating whisper. '*Sulking*! Just because I told him on the way here that if he *willed* to be well he *would* be well. It always annoyed him, but I must be true to my principles, mustn't I? – Even if it makes him *sulk* – *even* if he cuts me out of his will I must—'

'Hush, Frederica! He'll hear you!'

'No, dear, he's almost stone deaf.'

She leant down again to his ear.

'Is your DEAFNESS any better, Uncle George?' she screamed.

She seemed to regard Uncle George as her own special property.

William growled again.

'YOU REMEMBER MOTHER, DEAR UNCLE GEORGE, DON'T YOU?' FREDERICA SCREAMED INTO THE MUFFLER. WILLIAM MERELY GROWLED.

The circle drew another step farther back. The old lady looked anxious.

'I'm afraid he's ill,' she said. 'I hope it's nothing infectious! James, I think you'd better examine him.'

THEY ALL SURVEYED THE OCCUPANT OF THE BATH-CHAIR
WITH GREAT INTEREST.

Frederica drew one of the bashful and unwilling young
men forward.

'This is your great-nephew, James,' she shouted, 'DEAR

Uncle George. He's a MEDICAL STUDENT, and he'd SO love to talk to you.'

The rest withdrew to the other end of the lawn and watched proceedings from a distance. It would be difficult to say whether James or William felt the more desperate.

'Er – how are you, Uncle George?' said James politely, then, remembering Uncle George's deafness, changed his soft bass to a shrill tenor. 'HOW ARE YOU?'

William did not answer. He was wondering how long it would be before one of them tore off his rug and muffler and horn-rimmed spectacles, and hoping that it would not be either of the young men who would administer punishment.

'Er – may I – er – feel your pulse?' went on James, then remembered and yelled 'PULSE'.

William sat on his hands and growled. James mopped his brow.

'If I could see your tongue – er – TONGUE – you seem to be in pain – perhaps – TONGUE – allow me.'

He took hold of the muffler about William's head. William gave a sudden shake and a fierce growl and James started back as though he had been bitten. William was certainly perfecting the growl.

It was gaining a note of savage, almost blood-curdling ferocity. James gazed at him apprehensively, then, as another growl began to arise from the depth of William's chair, hastily rejoined the others.

'I've – er – examined him,' he said, making a gesture as though to loosen his collar, and still gazing apprehensively in the direction of Uncle George. 'I've – er – examined him. There's nothing – er – fundamentally wrong with him. He's just – er – got a foul temper, that's all.'

'It is a case for you, then, I think, Jonathan,' said the old lady grimly.

Frederica drew the second reluctant youth across the lawn.

'This is your great-nephew Jonathan,' she yelled into the muffler. 'He's in the CHURCH. He's looking forward SO much to a TALK with you, DEAR Uncle George.'

With a sprightly nod at the horn-rimmed spectacles, she departed. Jonathan smiled mirthlessly. Then he proceeded to shout at William with *sotto voce* interjections.

'GOOD AFTERNOON, UNCLE GEORGE – confound you – WE'RE SO GLAD TO SEE YOU – don't think – WE EXPECT TO SEE A LOT OF YOU NOW – worse luck – WE WANT TO BE A HAPPY, UNITED FAMILY – you crusty old mummy – WE HOPE – er – WE HOPE – er—'

He couldn't think what else to hope, so, purple with the effort of shouting, he stopped for breath. William, who was enjoying this part, chuckled. Jonathan with a sigh of relief departed. He went to the others who were watching expectantly.

'It's all right,' he said airily. 'The old chap's quite good-tempered now. My few words seemed to hit the spot.'

William watched the group, wondering what was going to be done next and who was going to do it. He hardly dared move in case his spectacles or muffler or rug fell off and revealed him to the cold light of day. He felt instinctively that the cold light of day would have little pity on him.

Then he saw two maids come round the house to the lawn. One carried a table and the other a tray on which were some cakes that made William's mouth water. Would he— oh, would he have to sit fasting and watch these unworthy people eat those glorious cakes? and – oh, scrummy! – there was a bowl of fruit salad. Surely—

Oh, surely he deserved a bit of food after all he'd been through. His eyes shone eagerly and hungrily through his horn-rimmed spectacles. If he just undid his muffler enough to eat a bit of fruit salad – and that chocolate cake – *and* the one with green icing – oh, *and* that one with nuts on the top – surely eating just a little like that wouldn't give him away. He couldn't starve for ever.

And what was going to happen to him, anyway? He couldn't stay all his life in a bath-chair in that garden starving and growling at people – he was jolly sick of it already, but he didn't know what to do – they'd have to find out sometime – and he didn't know what they'd do when they did find out – and he was sick of the whole thing – and it was all Ginger's fault going off and leaving him and— He looked across the lawn at them. His gaze through the horn-rimmed spectacles was wistful.

To his horror he saw Emmeline being launched across the lawn to him by Frederica. Emmeline wore a super-sweet expression and carried in her hand a bunch of roses. She laid them on the bath-chair with an artless and confiding smile.

'Dear, great great-Uncle George,' she said in her squeaky little voice. 'We're all so glad to see you and love you so much an'—'

The elders were watching the tableau with proud smiles, and William was summoning his breath for a really ferocious growl when suddenly everyone turned round. A little old man, purple with anger, had appeared running up the drive.

'Where is he?' screamed the little old man in fury. 'They said he came in here – my bath-chair – where is he? – The thief – the blackguard – how dare he? – I'll teach him – where is he?'

William did not wait to be taught. With admirable presence of mind he tore off his wrappings, flung away his horn-rimmed spectacles, and dashed with all his might through the opening in the hedge and across the back lawn. The little old man caught up a trowel that the gardener had left near a bed and flung it after William. It caught him neatly on the ankle and changed his swift flight to a limp.

'Dear Uncle George,' cooed Frederica to the old man, 'I don't know what's happened, but I *always* said you could walk quite well if you liked.'

With a howl of fury the old man turned on her, snatched up the bowl of fruit salad and emptied it over her.

Meanwhile the muscular young medical student had overtaken William just as he was disappearing through the gate and in spite of William's struggles was administering fairly adequate physical correction . . . Occasionally Nemesis did overtake William.

The next day William met Ginger on the way to school.

'Well, *you're* brave, aren't you?' he said sarcastically. 'Goin' off an' leavin' me an' not rescuin' me nor nothin'.'

'I like that,' said Ginger indignantly. 'What could I do, I'd like to know? You *would* ride an' me push. 'F you'd bin unselfish an' pushed an' me rode *you'd* 've got off.'

This was unanswerable, but while William was trying to think out an answer Ginger said scornfully:

'You still practisin' havin' a false leg? I stopped clickin' ever so long ago. I should think you was tired of that old game.'

'Well, I'm *not*!' said William with great self-possession. 'I'm goin' to go on some time yet jus' to show I *can*.'

Just then Emmeline appeared on the road, wearing the horn-rimmed spectacles.

'I say, those is ours!' said Ginger.

'Oh, *no*!' said Emmeline with a shrill triumphant laugh. 'I found them on our front lawn. They're *mine* now. You ask William Brown *how* I found them on our front lawn. But they're *mine* now. So there!'

For a moment William was nonplussed. Then a beatific smile overspread his freckled face.

'Dear great great-Uncle George!' he mimicked in a shrill falsetto. 'We're all so glad to see you – we love you so much.'

Emmeline gave a howl of anger and ran down the road holding her horn-rimmed spectacles on as she ran.

'Boo-hoo!' she sobbed. '*Nasty* William Brown! Comin'
into our garden an' breathin' our air an' runnin' over our
beds an' makin' Uncle George cross an' wastin' our fruit
salad an' bein' nasty to me – *Nasty* William Brown –
they're my spectacles, they is – Boo-hoo!'

'I say, what happened yesterday?' said Ginger when she
had disappeared.

'Oh, I almost forget,' said William evasively. 'I growled
at 'em an' scared 'em no end an' I didn't get any tea an' he
threw somethin' at me' – Oh, a lot of things like that – I
almost forget – But,' with sudden interest, 'how much did
she give you?'

'Sixpence,' said Ginger proudly, taking it out of his
pocket.

'Come on!' said William joyfully, giving a cheerful
little limp forward. 'Come on an' let's spend it.'

CHAPTER 13

WILLIAM AND SAINT VALENTINE

William was, as not infrequently, under a cloud. His mother had gone to put some socks into one of his bedroom drawers and had found that most of the drawer space was occupied by insects of various kinds, including a large stag beetle, and that along the side of the drawer was their larder, consisting of crumby bits of bread and a little pool of marmalade.

'But it *eats* marmalade,' pleaded William. 'The stag beetle does. I know it does. The marmalade gets a little less every day.'

'Because it's soaking into the wood,' said Mrs Brown sternly. '*That's* why. I don't know why you *do* such things, William!'

'But they're doing no harm,' said William. 'They're *friends* of mine. They *know* me. The stag beetle does anyway and the others will soon. I'm teaching the stag beetle tricks . . . *Honest*, it knows me and it knows its name. Call "Albert" to it and see if it moves.'

'I shall do nothing of the sort, William. Take the

creatures out at once. I shall have to scrub the drawers and have everything washed. You've got marmalade and crumbs all over your socks and handkerchiefs.'

'Well, I moved 'em right away when I put them in. They've sort of spread back.'

'Why ever didn't you keep the things outside?'

'I wanted to have 'em and play with 'em at nights an' mornin's.'

'And here's one of them *dead*!'

'I hope it didn't die of anythin' catchin',' said William anxiously. 'I shun't like Albert to get anythin'. There's no *reason* for 'em to die. They've got plenty of food an' plenty of room to play about in an' air gets in through the keyhole.'

'Take them *away*!'

William lovingly gathered up his stag beetle and woodlice and centipedes and earwigs and took them downstairs, leaving his mother groaning over the crumby marmalady drawer . . .

He put them into cardboard boxes and punched holes in the tops. He put Albert, the gem of the collection, in a small box in his pocket.

Then it began to rain and he came back to the house.

There was nothing to do . . .

He wandered from room to room. No one was in. The

only sounds were the sounds of the rain and of his mother furiously scrubbing at the drawer upstairs. He wandered into the kitchen. It was empty. On the table by the window was a row of jam jars freshly filled and covered. His mother had made jam that morning. William stood by the table, half sprawling over it, resting his head on his hands and watched the rain disconsolately. There was a small knife on the table. William took it up and, still watching the rain, absent-mindedly 'nicked' in all the taut parchment covers one by one. He was thinking of Albert. As he nicked in the parchment, he was vaguely conscious of a pleasant sensation like walking through heaped-up fallen leaves or popping fuchsia buds or breaking ice or treading on nice fat acorns . . . He was vaguely sorry when the last one was 'nicked'.

Then his mother came in.

'*William!*' she screamed as she saw the jam jars.

'What've I done now?' said William innocently. 'Oh . . . those! I jus' wasn't thinking what I was doin'. Sorry!'

Mrs Brown sat down weakly on a kitchen chair.

'I don't think anyone ever had a boy like you ever before, William,' she said with deep emotion. 'The work of *hours* . . . And it's *after* time for you to get ready for Miss Lomas's class. Do go, and then perhaps I'll get a little peace!'

*

Miss Lomas lived at the other end of the village. She held a Bible class for the Sons and Daughters of Gentlefolk every Saturday afternoon. She did it entirely out of the goodness of her heart, and she had more than once regretted the goodness of her heart since that Son of Gentlefolk known to the world as William Brown had joined her class. She had worked hard to persuade Mrs Brown to send him. She thought that she could influence William for good. She realised when William became a regular attendant of her class that she had considerably overestimated her powers. William could only be persuaded to join the class because most of his friends, not without much exertion of maternal authority, went there every Saturday. But something seemed to have happened to the class since William joined it. The beautiful atmosphere was destroyed. No beautiful atmosphere was proof against William. Every Saturday Miss Lomas hoped that something would have happened to William so that he could not come, and every Saturday William hoped equally fervently that something would have happened to Miss Lomas so that she could not take the class. There was something dispirited and hopeless in their greeting of each other . . .

William took his seat in the dining-room where Miss

Lomas always held her class. He glanced round at his fellow students, greeting his friends Ginger and Henry and Douglas with a hideous contortion of his face . . .

Then he took a large nut out of his pocket and cracked it with his teeth.

'*Not* in here, William,' said Miss Lomas faintly.

'I was goin' to put the bits of shell into my pocket,' said William. 'I wasn't goin' to put 'em on your carpet or anything, but 'f you don't want me to's all right,' he said obligingly, putting nut and dismembered shell into his pocket.

'Now we'll say our verses,' said Miss Lomas brightly but keeping a fascinated apprehensive eye on William. 'William, you begin.'

''Fraid I din't learn 'em,' said William very politely. 'I was goin' to last night an' I got out my Bible an' I got readin' 'bout Jonah in the whale's belly an' I thought maybe it'd do me more good than St Stephen's speech an' it was ever so much more int'restin'.'

'That will do, William,' said Miss Lomas. 'We'll – er – all take our verses for granted this afternoon, I think. Now, I want to give you a little talk on Brotherly Love.'

'Who's Saint Valentine?' said William who was burrowing in his prayer book.

. 'Why, William?' said Miss Lomas patiently.

'Well, his day seems to be comin' this month,' said William.

Miss Lomas, with a good deal of confusion, launched into a not very clear account of the institution of Saint Valentine's Day.

'Well, I don't think much of *him*'s a saint,' was William's verdict, as he took out another nut and absentmindedly cracked it, 'writin' soppy letters to girls instead of gettin' martyred prop'ly like Peter an' the others.'

Miss Lomas put her hand to her head.

'You misunderstand me, William,' she said. 'What I meant to say was— Well, suppose we leave Saint Valentine till later, and have our little talk on Brotherly Love first . . . *Ow-w-w*!'

Albert's box had been accidentally opened in William's pocket, and Albert was now discovered taking a voyage of discovery up Miss Lomas's jumper. Miss Lomas's spectacles fell off. She tore Albert off and rushed from the room.

William gathered up Albert and carefully examined him. 'She might have hurt him, throwing him about like that,' he said sternly. 'She oughter be more careful.'

Then he replaced Albert tenderly in his box.

'Give us a nut,' said Ginger.

Soon all the Sons and Daughters of Gentlefolk were cracking nuts, and William was regaling them with a racy account of Jonah in the whale's belly, and trying to entice Albert to show off his tricks . . .

'Seems to me,' said William at last thoughtfully, looking round the room, 'we might get up a good game in this room . . . something sort of quiet, I mean, jus' till she comes back.'

But the room was mercifully spared one of William's 'quiet' games by the entrance of Miss Dobson, Miss Lomas's cousin, who was staying with her. Miss Dobson was very young and very pretty. She had short golden curls and blue eyes and small white teeth and an attractive smile.

'My cousin's not well enough to finish the lesson,' she said. 'So I'm going to read to you till it's time to go home. Now, let's be comfortable. Come and sit on the hearthrug. That's right. I'm going to read to you *Scalped by the Reds.*'

William drew a breath of delight.

At the end of the first chapter he had decided that he wouldn't mind coming to this sort of Bible class every day.

At the end of the second he had decided to marry Miss Dobson as soon as he grew up . . .

When William woke up the next morning his determination to marry Miss Dobson was unchanged. He had

271

previously agreed quite informally to marry Joan Crewe, his friend and playmate and adorer, but Joan was small and dark haired and rather silent. She was not gloriously grown-up and tall and fair and vivacious. William was aware that marriage must be preceded by courtship, and that courtship was an arduous business. It was not for nothing that William had a sister who was acknowledged to be the beauty of the neighbourhood, and a brother who was generally involved in a passionate if short-lived *affaire d'amour*. William had ample opportunities of learning how it was done. So far he had wasted these opportunities or only used them in a spirit of mockery and ridicule, but now he determined to use them seriously and to the full.

He went to the garden shed directly after breakfast and discovered that he had made the holes in his cardboard boxes rather too large and the inmates had all escaped during the night. It was a blow, but William had more serious business on hand than collecting insects. And he still had Albert. He put his face down to where he imagined Albert's ear to be and yelled 'Albert' with all the force of his lungs. Albert moved – in fact scuttled wildly up the side of his box.

'Well, he cert'n'ly knows his name now,' said William with a sigh of satisfaction. 'It's took enough trouble to teach him that. I'll go on with tricks now.'

He went to school after that. Albert accompanied him, but was confiscated by the French master just as William and Ginger were teaching him a trick. The trick was to climb over a pencil, and Albert, who was labouring under a delusion that freedom lay beyond the pencil, was picking it up surprisingly well. William handed him to the French master shut up in his box, and was slightly comforted for his loss by seeing the master on opening it get his fingers covered with Albert's marmalade ration for the day, which was enclosed in the box with Albert. The master emptied Albert out of the window and William spent 'break' in fruitless search for him, calling 'Albert!' in his most persuasive tones . . . in vain, for Albert had presumably returned to his mourning family for a much needed 'rest cure'.

'Well, *I* call it stealin',' said William sternly, 'takin' beetles that belong to other people . . . It'd serve 'em right if I turned a Bolshevist.'

'I don't suppose they'd mind what you turned,' said Ginger unfeelingly but with perfect truth.

It was a half-holiday that afternoon, and to the consternation of his family William announced his intention of staying home instead of, as usual, joining his friends the Outlaws in their lawless pursuits.

'But, William, some people are coming to tea,' said Mrs Brown helplessly.

'I know,' said William. 'I thought p'raps you'd like me to be in to help with 'em.'

The thought of this desire for William's social help, attributed to her by William, left Mrs Brown speechless. But Ethel was not speechless.

'Well, of course,' she remarked to the air in front of her, 'that means that the whole afternoon is spoilt.'

William could think of no better retort to this than: 'Oh, yes, it does, does it? Well I never!'

Though he uttered these words in a tone of biting sarcasm and with what he fondly imagined to be a sarcastic smile, even William felt them to be rather feeble and added hastily in his normal manner:

''Fraid I'll eat up all the cakes, I s'pose? Well, I will if I get the chance.'

'William, dear,' said Mrs Brown, roused to effort by the horror of the vision thus called up, 'do you think it's quite fair to your friends to desert them like this? It's the only half-holiday in the week, you know.'

'Oh, 's all right,' said William. 'I've told 'em I'm not comin'. They'll get on all right.'

'Oh, yes, *they'll* be all right,' said Ethel in a meaningful voice and William could think of no adequate reply.

But William was determined to be at home that afternoon. He knew that Laurence Hinlock, Ethel's latest admirer, was expected and William wished to study at near quarters the delicate art of courtship. He realised that he could not marry Miss Dobson for many years to come, but he did not see why his courtship of her should not begin at once . . . He was going to learn how it was done from Laurence Hinlock and Ethel . . .

He spent the earlier part of the afternoon collecting a few more insects for his empty boxes. He was still mourning bitterly the loss of Albert. He deliberately did not catch a stag beetle that crossed his path because he was sure that it was not Albert. He found an earwig that showed distinct signs of intelligence and put it in a large, airy box with a spider for company and some leaves and crumbs and a bit of raspberry jam for nourishment. He did not give it marmalade because marmalade reminded him so poignantly of Albert . . .

Then he went indoors. There were several people in the drawing-room. He greeted them rather coldly, his eye roving round the while for what he sought. He saw it at last . . . Ethel and a tall, lank young man sitting in the window alcove in two comfortable chairs, talking vivaciously and confidentially. William took a chair from the wall and carried it over to them, put it down by the young man's chair, and sat down.

There was a short, pregnant silence.

'Good afternoon,' said William at last.

'Er – good afternoon,' said the young man. There was another silence.

'Hadn't you better go and speak to the others?' said Ethel.

'I've spoke to them,' said William.

There was another silence.

'Don't you want to go and play with your friends?' asked the young man.

'No, thank you,' said William.

Silence again.

'I think Mrs Franks would like you to go and talk to her,' said Ethel.

'No, I don't think she would,' said William with perfect truth.

The young man took out a shilling and handed it to William.

'Go and buy some sweets for yourself,' he said.

William put the shilling in his pocket.

'Thanks,' he said. 'I'll go and get them tonight when you've all gone.'

There was another and yet deeper silence. Then Ethel and the young man began to talk together again. They had evidently decided to ignore William's presence. William

276

listened with rapt attention. He wanted to know what you said and the sort of voice you said it in.

'St Valentine's Day next week,' said Laurence soulfully.

'Oh, no one takes any notice of that nowadays,' said Ethel.

'I'm going to,' said Laurence. 'I think it's a beautiful idea. Its meaning, you know . . . true love . . . If I send you a Valentine, will you accept it?'

'That depends on the Valentine,' said Ethel with a smile.

'It's the thought that's behind it that's the vital thing,' said Laurence soulfully. 'It's that that matters. Ethel . . . you're in all my waking dreams.'

'I'm sure I'm not,' said Ethel.

'You are . . . Has anyone told you before that you're a perfect Botticelli?'

'Heaps of people,' said Ethel calmly.

'I was thinking about love last night,' said Laurence. 'Love at first sight. That's the only sort of love . . . When first I saw you my heart leapt at the sight of you.' Laurence was a great reader of romances. 'I think that we're predestined for each other. We must have known each other in former existences. We—'

'Do speak up,' said William irritably. 'You're speaking so low that I can't hear what you're saying.'

'DON'T YOU WANT TO GO AND PLAY WITH YOUR FRIENDS?'
ASKED THE YOUNG MAN.

'*What?*'

The young man turned a flaming face of fury on to
him. William returned his gaze quite unabashed.

'I don' mean I want you to *shout*,' said William, 'but
just speak so's I can hear.'

'NO, THANK YOU,'
SAID WILLIAM.

The young man turned to Ethel.

'Can you get a wrap and come into the garden?' he said.

'Yes . . . I've got one in the hall,' said Ethel, rising.

William fetched his coat and patiently accompanied them round the garden.

'What do people mean by sayin' they'll send a Valentine, Mother?' said William that evening. 'I thought he was a sort of saint. I don' see how you can send a saint to anyone, specially when he's dead 'n' in the Prayer Book.'

'Oh, it's just a figure of speech, William,' said Mrs Brown vaguely.

'A figure of what?' said William blankly.

'I mean, it's a kind of Christmas card only it's a Valentine, I mean . . . Well, it had gone out in my day, but I remember your grandmother showing me some that

279

had been sent to her . . . dried ferns and flowers pasted on cardboard . . . very pretty.'

'Seems sort of silly to me,' said William after silent consideration.

'People were more romantic in those days,' said Mrs Brown with a sigh.

'Oh, I'm romantic,' said William, 'if that means bein' in love. I'm that all right. But I don' see any sense in sendin' pasted ferns an' dead saints and things . . . But still,' determinedly, 'I'm goin' to do all the sort of things they do.'

'What *are* you talking about, William?' said Mrs Brown.

Then Ethel came in. She looked angrily at William.

'Mother, William behaved abominably this afternoon.'

'I thought he was rather good, dear,' said Mrs Brown mildly.

'What did I do wrong?' said William with interest.

'Followed us round everywhere listening to everything we said.'

'Well, I jus' listened, din' I?' said William rather indignantly. 'I din' interrupt 'cept when I couldn't hear or couldn't understand. There's nothing wrong with jus' *listenin'*, is there?'

'But we didn't *want* you,' said Ethel furiously.

'Oh . . . that!' said William. 'Well, I can't help people not *wanting* me, can I? That's not *my* fault.'

Interest in Saint Valentine's Day seemed to have infected the whole household. On February 13th William came upon his brother Robert wrapping up a large box of chocolates.

'What's that?' said William.

'A Valentine,' said Robert shortly.

'Well, Miss Lomas said it was a dead Saint, and Mother said it was a pasted fern, an' now you start sayin' it's a box of chocolates! No one seems to know what it is. Who's it for, anyway?'

'Doreen Dobson,' said Robert, answering without thinking and with a glorifying blush.

'Oh, I *say*!' said William indignantly. 'You can't. I've bagged her. I'm going to do a fern for her. I've had her ever since the Bible Class.'

'Shut up and get out,' said Robert.

Robert was twice William's size.

William shut up and got out.

The Lomas family was giving a party on Saint Valentine's Day, and William had been invited with Robert and Ethel. William spent two hours on his Valentine. He could not find a fern, so he picked a large spray of yew-tree instead. There was no time to dry it, so he tried to affix it to paper as it was. At first he tried with a piece of notepaper and flour and water, but except for a generous coating of himself with the paste there was no result. The yew refused to yield to treatment. It was too strong and too large for its paper. Fortunately, however, he found a large piece of thick cardboard, about the size of a drawing-board, and a bottle of glue in the cupboard of his father's writing desk. It took the whole bottle of glue to fix the spray of yew-tree on to the cardboard, and the glue mingled freely with the flour and water on William's clothing and person. Finally he surveyed his handiwork.

'Well, I don' see much *in* it now it's done,' he said, 'but I'm jolly well going to do all the things they do do.'

He went to put on his overcoat to hide the ravages beneath, and met Mrs Brown in the hall.

'Why are you wearing your coat, dear?' she said solicitously. 'Are you feeling cold?'

'No. I'm just getting ready to go out to tea. That's all,' said William.

'But you aren't going out to tea for half an hour or so yet.'

'No, but you always say that I ought to start gettin' ready in good time,' said William virtuously.

'Yes, of course, dear. That's very thoughtful of you,' said Mrs Brown, touched.

William spent the time before he started to the party inspecting his insect collection. He found that the spider had escaped and the earwig was stuck fast in the raspberry jam. He freed it, washed it, and christened it 'Fred'. It was beginning to take Albert's place in his affections.

Then he set off to Miss Lomas's carrying his Valentine under his arm. He started out before Ethel and Robert because he wanted to begin his courtship of Miss Dobson before anyone else was in the field.

Miss Lomas opened the door. She paled slightly as she saw William.

'Oh . . . William,' she said without enthusiasm.

'I've come to tea,' William said, and added hastily, 'I've been invited.'

'You're rather early,' said Miss Lomas.

'Yes, I thought I'd come early so's to be sure to be in time,' said William, entering and wiping his feet on the mat. 'Which room're we goin' to have tea in?'

With a gesture of hopelessness Miss Lomas showed him into the empty drawing-room.

'It's Miss Dobson I've really come for,' explained William obligingly as he sat down.

Miss Lomas fled, but Miss Dobson did not appear.

William spent the interval wrestling with his Valentine. He had carried it sticky side towards his coat, and it now adhered closely to him. He managed at last to tear it away, leaving a good deal of glue and bits of yew-tree still attached to his coat . . . No one came . . . He resisted the temptation to sample a plate of cakes on a side table, and amused himself by pulling sticky bits of yew off his coat and throwing them into the fire from where he sat. A good many landed on the hearthrug. One attached itself to a priceless Chinese vase on the mantelpiece. William looked at what was left of his Valentine with a certain dismay. Well . . . he didn't call it pretty, but if it was the sort of thing they did he was jolly well going to do it . . . That was all . . . Then the guests began to arrive, Robert and Ethel among the first. Miss Dobson came in with Robert. He handed her a large box of chocolates.

'A Valentine,' he said.

'Oh . . . thank you,' said Miss Dobson, blushing.

William took up his enormous piece of gluey cardboard with bits of battered yew adhering at intervals.

'A Valentine,' he said.

Miss Dobson looked at it in silence. Then:

'W-what is it, William?' she said faintly.

'A Valentine,' repeated William shortly, annoyed at its reception.

'WHAT IS IT, WILLIAM?' ASKED MISS DOBSON.
'A VALENTINE,' REPEATED WILLIAM. 'MY VALENTINE.'

'Oh,' said Miss Dobson.

Robert led her over to the recess by the window which contained two chairs. William followed, carrying his chair. He sat down beside them. Both ignored him.

'Quite a nice day, isn't it?' said Robert.

'Isn't it?' said Miss Dobson.

'Miss Dobson,' said William, 'I'm always dreamin' of you when I'm awake.'

'What a pretty idea of yours to have a Valentine's Day party,' said Robert.

'Do you think so?' said Miss Dobson coyly.

'Has anyone ever told you that you're like a bottled cherry?' said William doggedly.

'Do you know . . . this is the first Valentine I've ever given anyone?' said Robert.

Miss Dobson lowered her eyes.

'Oh . . . is it?' she said.

'I've been thinkin' about love at first sight,' said William monotonously. 'I got such a fright when I saw you first. I think we're pre-existed for each other.'

'Will you allow me to take you out in my sidecar tomorrow?' said Robert.

'Oh, how lovely!' said Miss Dobson.

'No . . . pre-destinated . . . that's it,' said William. Neither of them took any notice of him. He felt depressed and disillusioned. She wasn't much of a catch anyway. He didn't know why he'd ever bothered about her.

'Quite a lady-killer, William,' said General Moult from the hearthrug.

'Beg pardon?' said William.

'I say you're a lady-killer.'

'I'm not,' said William, indignant at the aspersion. 'I've never killed no ladies.'

'I mean you're fond of ladies.'

'I think insects is nicer,' said William dispiritedly.

He was quiet for a minute or two. No one was taking any notice of him. Then he took up his Valentine, which was lying on the floor, and walked out.

The Outlaws were in the old barn. They greeted William joyfully. Joan, the only girl member, was there with them. William handed her his cardboard.

'A Valentine,' he said.

'What's a Valentine?' said Joan who did not attend Miss Lomas's class.

'Some say it's a saint what wrote soppy letters to girls 'stead of gettin' martyred prop'ly, like Peter an' the others, an' some say it's a bit of fern like this, an' some say it's a box of chocolates.'

'Well, I never!' said Joan surprised. 'But it's beautiful of you to give it to me, William.'

'It's a jolly good piece of cardboard,' said Ginger, ''f we scrape away these messy leaves an' stuff.'

William joined with zest in the scraping.

287

'How's Albert?' said Joan.

After all there was no one quite like Joan. He'd never contemplate marrying anyone else ever again.

'He's been took off me,' said William.

'Oh, what a *shame*, William!'

'But I've got another . . . an earwig . . . called Fred.'

'I'm so glad.'

'But I like you better than *any* insect, Joan,' he said generously.

'Oh, William, do you *really*?' said Joan, deeply touched.

'Yes – an I'm goin' to marry you when I grow up if you won't want me to talk a lot of soppy stuff that no one can understand.'

'Oh, thank you, William . . . No, I won't.'

'All right . . . Now come on an' let's play Red Indians.'

Read them all!

Just William

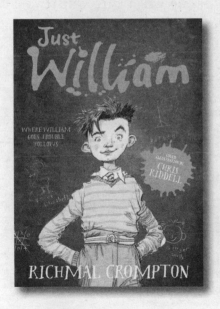

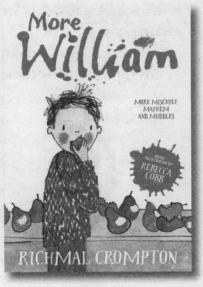

Read them all!

Just William

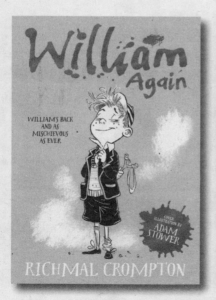